"I'm coming wi

"All right," he agre
From this moment

"And if I don't?" She
forcing herself to lo   dark eyes.

He took a step toward her, until his large, intimidating body was just a whisper apart from hers. She stopped breathing.

"You don't scare me, Ashford Stanton..."

He grinned then, a slow, seductive smile, and her heart began to clamor, ricocheting in her chest. She had never seen him smile properly before... and wow. She felt her legs begin to tremble again.

And now she knew she was lying to him and herself, because he was the most overwhelmingly attractive man she had ever seen, and they were all alone out here in the forest, just the two of them. The truth was, it scared her to death.

SARAH RODI

Escaping with Her Saxon Enemy

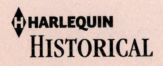

Sarah Rodi has always been a hopeless romantic. She grew up watching old romantic movies recommended by her grandad or devouring love stories from the local library. Sarah lives in the village of Cookham in Berkshire, UK, where she enjoys walking along the River Thames with her husband, her two daughters and their dog. She has been a magazine journalist for over twenty years, but it has been her lifelong dream to write romance for Harlequin. Sarah believes everyone deserves to find their happy-ever-after. You can contact her via @sarahrodiedits or sarahrodiedits@gmail.com.

Books by Sarah Rodi

Harlequin Historical

The Viking's Stolen Princess
Escaping with Her Saxon Enemy

Visit the Author Profile page
at Harlequin.com.

Chapter One

Kald Fortress, autumn 821

The bride and her entourage were late.

Ashford Stanton tried to curb his impatience by taking a deep, steadying breath and telling himself it didn't matter. It had been a long summer since he'd first seen her on the battlefield, and even though that day had affected him more than it should, her late arrival on this unusually warm afternoon had no right to bother him. He hated that it did.

Scanning his surroundings on the sheltered, windless beach, he made sure once again that nothing was amiss, that King Eallesborough was safe and everything was as it should be. Although nothing about this day could be described as ordinary. The excitement in the air was so thick he could almost reach out and grasp it, and Ash realised he was about to bear witness to a significant moment in history. If only his father was here to document it in his chronicles.

did not need. Which was why he was so eager for the wedding party to make an appearance—he needed to prove to himself that he would see the Danish shield maiden again and not feel a thing. He had positioned himself at the end of a row, where he could keep an eye on the people arriving, but he was only waiting for one.

Just at that moment a loud swell of rousing music announced the bride's entrance, and he rolled his shoulders, composing himself, before slowly turning around to look.

The bride glided past him to the altar and his lips twisted. He was actually glad his father couldn't be here to see such an occasion—he was already in ill health, and it might just have been the death of him. He had never thought he'd see the day when a Saxon princess would be married off to a Northman to form an alliance to keep the peace.

The possibility that this union had the potential to change perceptions and reshape Ash's own world hadn't passed him by, but he instantly banished the thought from his mind. There were a few secrets that were better left buried, so no one could get hurt.

Throughout his upbringing Ash's parents had told him stories about the Northmen's abhorrent invasions of Saxon castles and monasteries, destroying everything in their sights, raping and pillaging as they went. Those raiders came from faraway lands, navigating perilous oceans to land on Saxon beaches, take what they wanted from defenceless settlements and leave a trail of destruction in their wake. He had

spine in a mixture of intricate braids, curls and flowers that swayed as she moved. She had eyes like the ocean—deep-set, blue and wild—and skin as silky-smooth and pale as the sand beneath her bare feet.

She was a natural beauty, with her slender curves strapped into that close-fitting dress, and yet he knew she was strong. He'd seen her handle a sword and shield and it was a vision he'd struggled to erase from his memory these past few months.

He'd never seen a woman wield a blade before, and he'd been enthralled. He still was. Yet he knew he should not be. He didn't *want* to be.

As Svea moved towards him her piercing gaze lifted to his and a shot of awareness bolted through him, igniting a fresh pulse of desire. But just as quickly as their eyes met hers iced over, her back stiffened and she turned away.

He made a fist with his hand. Svea didn't even like him, and had never tried to hide it—not since the day he'd met her and told her to 'show mercy' on the battlefield. He would just have to stamp out this attraction, regain the control he was renowned for.

He would never forget the barbaric fight between her brother and Lord Crowe, the leader of a mercenary Saxon force... It had been one of the most brutal fights he'd ever witnessed, heightened by Svea charging forward at the final moment, ready to help her brother and run her sword through their enemy.

Stunned, Ash had stepped in and demanded she stop. He hadn't known what he knew now—that Crowe had killed their father. And although he un-

A *Danish* woman, who had hated him at first sight and would probably try to kill him if he ever made a move. Not that he was going to. He just had to get through tonight, and then he and his men would be leaving this place for good. He would never have to see her again.

He sat up straight in his seat, all too aware that she was drawing closer, pouring ale for his men, and any moment now would reach his table. He schooled his face in anticipation.

She stopped short when she saw him, as if deciding to take a different route around the hall, even looked as if she might stalk past him. It was nothing new. Due to his fierce reputation and formidable looks, people always kept their distance. He'd learned to live with it, even welcomed it, yet now it irritated him. Perhaps that was what had him opening his mouth, calling out to her...

'Svea.'

She seemed to waver, to consider ignoring him, and then obviously thought better of being so rude, and finally forced herself to turn towards him. He felt another punch to his gut when her beautiful blue eyes reached his.

'Ah, Lord Stanton. Would you care for a drink?' She held up the jug. 'I don't think I've seen you touch a drop all evening.'

Her narrow nose drew his gaze down and he studied her full, soft lips, which were a pretty petal-pink, although her smile looked stiff and her voice was clipped.

Her eyes flashed in the flickering firelight. Svea was headstrong, she was impetuous—she was everything he'd been brought up to see as dangerous in a person. And judging by the way his lower body was responding to hers, she was most certainly a danger to him...

'I'd waited years... I think that was long enough to consider my feelings on the matter.'

He sighed, but was careful to maintain his steady tone. 'I have had the man locked away—a satisfactory outcome for us both. Yet, if I'm not mistaken, you've avoided me each time we've met since.'

She shrugged one slim defined shoulder, unwittingly drawing his attention to the material of her dress stretching across the generous swells of her breasts. 'You flatter yourself, Lord Stanton. To ignore you would imply I am even aware of your presence.'

He clicked his jaw. He found her scorn irritating, but her indifference was maddening. Her hand on her hip, she gave him a challenging stare. His eyes dropped to her shoulder, where a dark, intricate design swirled its way over her collarbone and behind her hair. It looked like the twisted branches of a tree, winding up her neck. She had another dark symbol he didn't recognise etched into her wrist. He wanted to tug her closer and inspect it, but he didn't dare touch her. Her whole demeanour screamed for him to stay back.

'Some people may find your status as the King's right-hand man something to be lauded, but others

careful to keep them trained on her face. He knew how important it was to treat a woman with respect. 'Up until a moment ago, I thought you looked lovely.'

Her face darkened and she gave an unladylike disdainful snort. He wished the words back the moment he'd uttered them, knowing he'd made a mistake.

She placed the empty tankard down on his table. 'You seem to have a knack of imparting your opinion upon people who don't want to hear it, Lord Stanton. And, as I've been sweating like a pig on its way to the smokehouse all day, I think you should save your compliments for the bride.'

Svea abruptly turned and walked away from him, her dress swishing around her bare ankles, leaving him stunned once again. She wasn't like other women. He had certainly never met one who would scoff at a compliment, drink like a man, or wield a sword like a warrior. He'd never seen a woman with such patterns on her skin before. And no woman had ever spoken to him with such outright contempt. Well, except for his mother.

Svea didn't seem to care what people thought of her. She was just totally herself, and he envied her for that. He'd been ruled by honour, family reputation and others' opinions his whole life.

Was it his chastisement of her behaviour or the compliment that had had Svea stalking away from him? he wondered. Her anger at him seemed unwarranted, misdirected. After all, the man who had killed her father had been locked away, stripped of his wealth and titles. Ash himself had made sure of

to belong. Everything about him made her wary and she wasn't alone—even his men were mindful of him, in a respectful way, sensing it was safer to give him space. They were right.

Svea didn't want to go anywhere near him, and had even attempted to ignore him when he'd called out to her. She hadn't wanted to face him, lock eyes with him, or hear his patronising words. She felt on edge around him, as if he was judging her—probably because he was! He had expressed his stern disapproval of her behaviour the moment they'd met, and she had felt the censure in his deep brown eyes ever since.

Since her parents had died, no one apart from her brother had ever chastised her. How dare Lord Stanton think it was his place to do just that? Ridiculously, it made her want to rebel, to fight against it, to provoke him to react. It would certainly be interesting to crack that cool resolve of his.

The drinking of the bridal ale had gone on long into the night, and Svea had been careful to keep her distance from him, but she'd still imagined his dark, reprimanding gaze on her, following her as she went about her duties.

She had been shocked when he'd complimented her on her appearance, and it had caused a strange heat to flare in her stomach. She didn't seek, or want, any man's approval—least of all his! The men in Kald knew better than to comment on her looks. They saw her as one of them—a farmer, a fighter. It had taken years, and hard work on her part, to get to this posi-

wedding had been a mostly joyous occasion, but it had sought to remind her that she could never have what he had—fate had made sure she would never marry. As she'd watched his hands being bound to the Princess's during the ceremony, to signify that their lives were now tied to one another, she had known she would never belong to a man as his wife, that she could never be someone's property. Instead, she would continue to be a warrior and protector of Kald.

In marrying a Saxon princess Brand had helped to protect their lands and their people, through forging an alliance between Kald and Termarth, yet she had often wondered how he could love one of their kind, especially after what had happened to their father. *What had happened to her.* She could never be at ease in a Saxon's proximity.

Svea had been all too aware of the King's men at the wedding, yet she would never let them know they unnerved her. She wouldn't give anyone that satisfaction. She had learned to cover up her fear with a veneer of nonchalance and scorn, and so far it had served her well.

As she steered her horse to ride back down the hill towards the fortress, she was relieved to see the royal guard were readying their horses to leave, about to depart these shores for their own kingdom. Soon she would be able to breathe easily again.

Cantering back into the central square, she saw it was crowded with men in military dress, forcing her to slow her steed, Max. She took in the soldiers' glazed eyes and weary frames. It was clear the men

She'd wanted to lash out and attack his position, but he had a reputation for winning many battles, and a collection of face markings to rival those of any of Kald's warriors. Combat scars from fighting her own kind, perhaps? But, unlike her brother and the other Northmen she was accustomed to, Lord Stanton was impeccably dressed in full regalia and shiny chainmail, professing his loyalty to the crown.

'And what of your safety when we part ways? I cannot leave you unattended.'

'Your concern is unnecessary, Lord Stanton. Two of my men will be joining us, and they'll be only too happy to accompany me on the return journey.'

A muscle flickered in his proud face—the only sign that he might be irritated. She imagined he was used to getting his own way. Well, not today.

'All right. If you insist.' He glowered at her.

'I do.'

She turned in the saddle and sought out her men, Kar and Sten. She was secretly glad her Danish shield brothers were coming with her. It bolstered her confidence. Despite the fact that she'd tried to harden herself to situations like these over the years, she wouldn't normally choose to surround herself with so many Saxon men. It made her insides quiver.

'Bring up the rear,' she commanded them.

Spurring her horse into action, she took the lead as the convoy of Saxon soldiers began to depart the fortress. The sun was rising quickly in the grey sky, burning off the clouds ahead, and a sliver of excitement danced down her spine. Soon they would be

tive voice finally breaking the silence. 'I've never seen a woman ride astride before, rather than side-saddle.'

'Then you obviously haven't met a proper woman before, Lord Stanton.'

'I'm beginning to realise you are one of many talents...you ride, you drink, you fight—you even have control over your men. I'm impressed.'

'To impress you was far from my intent,' she said, rolling her eyes. She couldn't be sure if he was complimenting her or mocking her, and neither was acceptable to her.

'What's next for you, I wonder?' he added, ignoring her sarcasm.

She tipped her chin up. 'My brother has entrusted the fortress of Kald to my care while he's away, and I don't mean to let him down.'

His look of shocked surprise pleased her. Good. She wanted to confound him.

'And the men don't mind a woman being in charge?'

'I will see to it that the people of Kald are looked after and safe. I don't need any extra appendage for that, do I?'

His eyes narrowed on her. No doubt he didn't approve of her base words.

'You have your own fortress to rule over, do you not?' she continued.

He nodded tightly. 'It's my father's stronghold, actually.'

She had heard of the impressive garrison of Braewood, and of his father's deteriorating health, and she wondered why Lord Stanton spent his time in the ser-

tilted forward. 'What can you hear, boy? A deer or a fox, perhaps?'

'At this time of day? Doubtful,' Lord Stanton said, slowing his horse to pull up alongside her. 'You should be more careful, Svea.'

He scowled at her, before holding up his hand for his men to halt behind them. She swallowed down her irritation at his patronising tone. Who did he think he was?

He cocked his head, listening.

Max's ears twitched again and his nostrils flared. Her animal could detect danger. Svea knew it. She felt a trickle of unease flow through her as she used her hand to shield her eyes from the sun and scanned the horizon to see if she could see anything.

'Something's out there. Max is not easily frightened... He has good instincts.'

'As do I... I'll investigate.' Lord Stanton dismounted his horse and walked forward a few paces. 'Wait here.' His stern voice deepened, as if he meant to emphasise the instruction.

Svea shivered. She felt unsettled—as if she was being watched, as if she was waiting for something. But what? She searched their surroundings again. Apart from the braying of the horses and the murmurings of the men behind them, it was quiet. Too quiet.

She couldn't just sit here and do nothing. She jumped down after Lord Stanton, following him as he waded through the marsh.

He turned around and fixed her with a hard look. 'I told you to wait.'

splintering, as wave after wave of burly men lunged in their direction through the marsh.

She had put herself in the heart of battle many times, and she'd learnt how to hold her own. But that didn't prevent the intrusion of violent, upsetting memories of her past each time she came up against a male enemy. Driven by her need for self-protection, she sought strength from her darker emotions, her rage, in order to overcome the unwanted fear. She'd make these raiders sorry they'd ever attacked them.

Beside her, she was aware of Lord Stanton fighting, all too conscious of his powerful strength. His actions were fierce and deadly. No warrior was a match for his strength. She had never seen a man fight like that, with such lethal precision. She suddenly felt glad he was on her side.

It was all a blur of swords clashing and water splashing around their ankles. She fought off one man, then another. Her slight figure meant she was quicker and more nimble on her feet than most. Men were often shocked to see a woman fighting, and she used their surprise and hesitation for her gain.

What did these men want? Were they opportunists, or had they planned it, knowing the royal convoy would be travelling this way?

Back to back, she and Lord Stanton seemed to be making progress, warding off some of their attackers. Then, without warning, a giant of a man suddenly bore down on her, striking her in the face with his shield, and her sword clattered to the ground. She fell, landing on her back in the cold murky marsh, and he

'I'm fine,' she lied, fiercely pulling herself out of his grasp and reaching for her sword, which lay on the ground. 'I'm ready to fight again.'

'No!' he barked, taking her arm again with more force this time and dragging her backwards. 'Svea, look.'

She glanced round to see a shallow expanse of water now lay before them and their convoy—who were quickly being surrounded by the rest of the raiders who had charged out of the forest. And, to her horror, she saw that they were rounding up prisoners—the King included. She looked on in dismay as her men—her loyal friends who were usually so strong—reluctantly dropped their weapons in defeat.

'Quick. Come with me. This way,' Lord Stanton said, tugging her into the treeline, hiding them from view.

She struggled against his hold, trying to resist retreat. It went against every bone in her body to fall back, to surrender when people needed her help, when she'd been wronged. But Lord Stanton was too strong.

'What are you doing? We have to help the King… our men…'

She attempted to wrestle with him as he pulled her further into the dense forest. Rage ripped through her blood now, that ambushers had dared attack her, threaten her, and she wanted to fight back. She was so angry. And what was Lord Stanton doing? Why wasn't he fighting? Why was he sheathing his sword?

And why was his touch sending flames flickering across her skin?

been taken captive. She'd been attacked! And *he'd* saved her—a Saxon!

She swayed on her feet and he caught her by the elbow again.

'Are you sure you're all right?' he asked as he eased her down onto a fallen tree trunk.

'Don't touch me!' she spat.

'A woman like you shouldn't be fighting, Svea. You'll just be seen as bait—a temptation to these men. I told you not to come!'

Anger erupted inside her and she leapt back off the tree trunk, her face riotous. 'I'm as good a fighter as any of your men!'

A woman like you. She didn't like the vitriolic way he'd said it. What did he mean? Was her reputation at stake here?

The rage that had erupted inside her was quickly replaced by cold dread, and she ran her hand over the metal *kransen* around her arm. A symbol of her virginity. She felt a fraud for wearing it. But she was sure neither her brother nor his new wife would have said anything about her past...not to this man. Yes, he had been Princess Anne's guard before she'd married Brand, but he was still practically a stranger.

Feeling unsteady on her feet, she slumped back down again. She did not want to be seen as a *temptation*. Never. And the fact that he had described her as such—as bait—sent a warning signal through her. She had to get away from this man.

Lord Stanton seemed to have the opposite idea. He drew a hand over his face, as if to gather his thoughts,

Soon, she'd started to beat some of the men in Kald, who were twice her size and strength, in practice fights. And the day she'd bested Brand he'd scooped her up and whirled her round in the air as they'd grinned at each other in delight, knowing she was finally ready.

'He's taught you well. But you're putting yourself at risk, being out here among all these men. You must see that.'

He reached up and stroked a strand of hair from her face, attempting to tuck it behind her ear, but she stiffened, recoiling from his touch and casting him off with her arm.

'And now you're hurt.' He stood, nodding to her forehead.

She frowned, putting her fingers to her temple. She hadn't realised she was bleeding. She could not understand him. One moment he was chastising her, the next he was troubled by her plight.

'I'm fine…it's the others I'm worried about. Lord Stanton—'

'Ashford,' he said. 'That is my name. You can call me Ash.'

Ash. It suited him. She swallowed. 'We can't just leave them…'

'Of course not. I don't intend to,' he said, prowling over towards a clearing to peer through the trees.

Svea let out a breath she hadn't realised she'd been holding. She shook her head. 'Who are these men? What do they want?'

'I don't know. I don't recognise them.' He crouched quietly, observing like Fenrir, the giant black wolf

Her face shot up to his. 'Wait? Never! They're my men, too. I'm coming with you.'

She couldn't believe what she was saying. She didn't want to be alone with this man. She had sworn to hate him. She didn't know him, or what he was capable of. For all she knew he might have dragged her into the forest as a ruse to attack her.

With that thought in her mind she glanced around, checking her surroundings, looking for a place she could run and hide if she needed to. But she had never been afraid to take risks, and she couldn't just sit idly by while her men were in trouble. Lord Stanton was about to find out she could be just as assertive as him.

He shook his head. 'It's too dangerous. I'll be faster, and better, on my own. I can't vouch for your safety—'

Did he really care about that? 'I'm not asking you to protect me!' she bit out, interrupting him.

'Your brother would want me to make sure you are safe.'

She launched herself off the log and shook herself down, defying him, preparing to leave. 'I can fend for myself, and Brand knows it. He taught me how to do just that. Besides, we don't know what's waiting for us at Kald, either—if the fortress has been attacked.'

His dark eyes studied her, glowering. But her final comment seemed to sway him. He must have realised she was right. They didn't know if this was a two-pronged attack—if there were other men who had watched them leave Kald this morning, seen an opportunity and advanced upon the settlement...

Chapter Two

Ash cursed himself. He should have seen this coming.

Keeping low within the undergrowth so as not to draw any attention to themselves, they followed the convoy of captives along the forest edge for a while, throughout the midday sun, listening to the band of ambushers throwing insults at the King, the soldiers, but mainly the Danes.

Ash knew this wasn't good. He'd thought maybe they were opportunists, simple thieves, but the longer they trekked on, the more it seemed they had a destination—and a purpose—in mind.

He was angry with himself for letting his men drink too much ale last night. They would have been able to fight better with their wits about them. And he was even more furious with himself for agreeing to let Svea escort them to the forest. If he'd stood firm she would be safe at home right now. That was if Kald hadn't been attacked, too. But seeing her stand up to him this morning, dressed in body-tight armour,

was possible. He knew his imposing looks struck fear into many.

He had been momentarily in awe of her skills with a sword, impressed by her fearlessness—until she'd almost got herself killed. When he'd seen that man knock her to the ground, pressing her under the water with his weight and making lewd comments, Ash's blood had run cold. It had only confirmed his suspicions that having a woman on the battlefield was a terrible idea—especially one of such beauty. He was painfully aware of the reaction she could induce in men, and what beasts they could be. He'd suffered the ramifications of that kind of behaviour his whole life.

His fierce need to protect her had made him see red. His control had slipped and he'd dispatched those men in cold fury—no regrets. He didn't want to look too closely at that part of him—at what kind of blood ran through his veins to make him behave like that. He had been so determined not to let anything bad happen to her, he even wondered if he'd sacrificed the King's safety for her own. And yet, even though he knew he had failed in his duties, he couldn't bring himself to regret it. He would make the same choice again.

He couldn't understand why he felt so protective of her. He didn't want to feel this way. For a man of his standing to like a Danish woman—he was certain it would all but ruin his reputation. But still, he admired the way she'd handled herself, the way she'd been so brave, crushing her emotions, caring more about the safety of her men and her people back at Kald than the fact she'd been attacked herself.

Svea reached for the little leather water satchel from her armour, and when she took a huge swig, quenching her thirst, Ash ran his tongue over his lips. Hesitantly, she passed it to him, careful to evade his touch.

'Thanks.'

She looked like a different person from the feminine beauty who'd strolled through the hall towards him yesterday, her hair now plaited into tight braids and piled on top of her head, tight coils cascading down her back. Her face was streaked with dirt, her tunic was torn in places from the brambles and she had a nasty gash to her right temple. But she was no less attractive.

He liked the fact that she didn't conform—he found it intriguing. She was certainly unique in both her looks and her behaviour. And he knew he would have to start trying harder at fighting these disturbing feelings.

He reluctantly removed his tabard, which bore the banners of the crown, deciding it best to lose the royal colours in case they came across anyone and needed to go unnoticed. He tore a square from the material and soaked it in a nearby bubbling brook, squeezing it out before coming down beside Svea and pressing it against her forehead.

'You're still bleeding.'

She jerked away from him. 'I told you not to touch me! I can do it,' she said, wrinkling her nose, snatching the material from him.

He sighed. He wondered if they were really so

something like this would happen. He was insistent that I come to the wedding with him. A lot of people across the kingdom didn't agree with your brother marrying the Princess, and they certainly don't support the alliance between Termarth and Kald. It's caused a divide between the Saxon people.'

'Do you?'

'Do I what? Approve of a union between Danes and Saxons?' He shrugged. 'It doesn't really matter what I think.'

'You always seem to have an opinion on everything...'

His lips twisted. He prided himself on speaking his mind about all things bar his own family history.

'I like the idea that Termarth could become a place where all people would be welcomed.'

He wondered, in a place like that, if one day even he could be accepted for who he was. But first he'd have to learn to accept himself... He admired Brand and Anne for speaking out about their feelings, not caring what people thought of them. He wasn't sure he could ever do it, or subject himself to such scrutiny. Not when he knew just how hurtful it could be.

'When you have seen the things I have seen, it's hard to trust, to believe our people could live together.'

The accounts of Northmen raiding Saxon lands and then not leaving, but staying to create settlements, had become much more frequent lately. He knew the King hoped this marriage union would bring his people more security from these clans through forming

'You're right,' he conceded, inclining his head in acknowledgement. He realised he didn't know anything about her, and against his better judgement he wanted to. 'But I'm willing to learn. That must have been a terrible choice for your parents to make—and awful for you. You must miss your mother very much.'

He stretched out an arm to tug a few blackberries from the burgeoning hedgerow beside him and held them out to her. 'Are you hungry now?'

She leaned forward and he tipped them into her palm, his fingers brushing against hers, and the tiny touch triggered another ripple of awareness through his body.

'You have to admit, you are in the minority. Many of your kind come here looking for spoils or treasure,' he said.

'Well, we came looking for survival. We risked our lives in search of a new home. We're not what you think—we're not like some of the others. Kald was uninhabited when we arrived on these shores. We didn't steal anything—we just created a settlement and have found ourselves having to defend it ever since.'

Deep down, he already knew what she was saying to be true—her clan *wasn't* the same as the Northmen who had attacked Braewood all those years ago, who had done so much lasting damage to his home, his family...

Despite his innate hatred of her kind since childhood, he hadn't been able to eradicate his dark obsession with the Norse people. When he was just a boy,

she seemed unwilling to set aside their original dif-
fering views.

Ash inclined his head. 'You're talking about Lord
Crowe again.' It seemed she just couldn't let the subject die.

'Tell me, when you rode alongside him, did you
know what kind of man he was? What he was capable of?'

He sighed. 'I didn't know he'd killed your father,
if that's what you mean. And I still don't understand
why. Your brother said it was some kind of attack because you were Danes?'

She nodded and bit her lip.

Was there more to this than she was letting on?
he wondered again. He couldn't claim to be a fan of
her kind, but he would never attack someone just because they were a Dane. If Crowe had done that, it
really was despicable.

'I'm sorry. About your father.' He realised now
that the death of her father must have been even more
painful after losing her mother at such a young age.

'He was a good man.'

He nodded, and then, because he felt the need to
share something of himself, and to keep her talking,
he added, 'My mother died when I was young, too,
but of natural causes.'

It had been a strange day when he'd learnt of her
passing. He didn't remember feeling upset—he just
remembered his father's anger towards him, as if it
had somehow been Ash's fault. So he'd stayed away.
Ash had wished her back—of course he had. But he'd

port that had been built up between himself and the King and his men, meaning he would do all that he could to get them back. But having a sibling would have meant there would have been someone to soften his parents' scrutiny. Someone better placed than him to continue the Stanton line. But, no, his father had tasked him with the responsibility, and he'd threatened to deny Ash his inheritance, strip him of his lands and title, if he didn't comply.

'Married?'

He glanced up in surprise when she spoke, as if she was following his line of thought. 'No,' he said. 'I told you I wasn't keen on weddings.'

Of course there had been women over the years, but none of any significance. He was always careful to keep his emotions and his true self tightly locked away—for their sake more than his.

He saw the colour rise in her cheeks as she glanced away.

'I wasn't sure if that was because of a bad experience or just your lack of enjoyment of the festivities. You don't strike me as the kind of man who would enjoy a good celebration.'

'No?' He raised his eyebrows. 'I decided a long time ago never to marry or have children.'

It was for the best. All he wanted was to forge his own path in life—but because he'd been born into the Stanton family, that seemed impossible.

He hadn't heard from his father for years—until he had received word that Aethelbard had become ill and Ash was needed at home. He'd been called

proper home. He'd longed for the day when he could escape. And as soon as he'd been old enough he'd left. He'd returned to Braewood briefly, but he still hadn't been made to feel welcome, so he'd learned how to fight, taking his anger out on the battlefield, and worked his way up the ranks.

He'd thrived on the glory of winning, finally receiving the praise and accolades he'd always longed for as a child, and he had made his own success, becoming the King's loyal warrior through talent, not his family name, despite what Svea thought.

He glanced around, studying their surroundings. He admired the mature trees and listened to the soothing sounds of tumbling water. He felt at home in the wild like this, or out on the battlefield—not cooped up in some fortress, hosting feasts and ruling others. He knew he couldn't put off what his father was demanding of him forever, and yet even knowing this he was drawn back to his companion's face. Svea looked exhausted, her eyes heavy and her lips taut, and yet she was still achingly beautiful.

She avoided his gaze as she wrapped the cloak tighter around her. At least she hadn't refused that. He might not have to worry about her catching her death just yet.

'It's probably just as well you don't want to marry. I doubt anyone would have you anyway,' she mocked.

He grinned. 'You're so frosty, Svea. Is that why *you're* not married?'

Her eyes narrowed on him. 'I'm not married be-

soldiers must have taken the King as a hostage—to help Cecil rescue his brother.'

'See!' Svea fumed, rounding on him, a scowl carved into her beautiful features. 'You should have let me kill him when I had the chance. Then none of this would be happening.' She stabbed a finger into his chest. 'This is all your fault.'

He frowned, looking at the place where she'd jabbed him as if it burnt. Maybe she was right. Perhaps he should have let her avenge her father—at least then she wouldn't hate him so much, and the King might not have been captured.

He turned his attention back to the men, assessing the situation, wondering what they were planning.

'Do you think they'll demand an exchange? Crowe for the King?' Svea whispered, appalled.

He nodded. 'Possibly…'

Concern chilled him now. This was worse than he'd first thought. He felt certain they'd be heading to Termarth next—and at present the kingdom was at its weakest, with the King and some of Ash's best men having been taken hostage.'

'We need to do something,' Svea said. 'I know what Crowe is capable of. What if his brother is the same?'

And as if his worst fears were coming true, Ash watched as some men grabbed Kar and Sten and bundled them forward to stand before their leader. When he saw Cedric roll up his sleeves, a sneer carved into his face, the hairs on the back of his neck stood on end. This couldn't be good.

his arms wrapped around her back. She made every effort to free herself, her words muffled as he pressed her harder into his body.

'It'll be over in a moment,' he said. 'Keep quiet. Don't do anything foolish.'

Cedric continued to kick the Danish warrior and Svea stilled, her initial rage seeming to subside, but with each and every sickening blow she flinched in his arms. Ash ran his hands up and down her back, attempting to soothe her. She reminded him of a feral, frightened mare which had once bolted from Braewood's stables. He'd been tasked with talking her down, trying to get her to a safe enclosure.

After what seemed like aeons, the brutal beating finally stopped when Kar lay battered and bruised and still on the ground. 'It's all right. It's over,' Ash whispered, stroking Svea's hair. He fancied she almost leaned into him, or was that just wishful thinking? 'He's hurt, but he'll live.'

Svea suddenly pushed at his chest with her hands, staggering away from him, her face mutinous. 'You should have let me help him!' she fumed.

'You against all those men? You're crazy,' he said, disturbed by her behaviour.

Ash was barely holding his own annoyance at bay, furious with the Saxon men for their actions and his inability to help Kar, but just as angry with Svea for her extreme risk-taking yet again, and it took every shred of his resolve to carefully control his voice and tone.

'Evil runs through their blood,' she said bitterly. She ran her hands over her metal armband absent-mindedly.

He stared down at her. Did she really believe that such a thing was possible? That malice could run in a bloodline? If that was the case, what did it mean for him? He hoped it wasn't true. It was his worst fear.

He reached out to take her chin between his thumb and forefinger, lifting her beautiful blue gaze to his. 'We have to hope they're safe for now—at least until they get to Termarth, if that's where they're heading. It might just buy us some time to raise troops.'

'What are you suggesting?'

'That we go to Braewood and raise the *fyrd*— an army of free men willing to fight for the King. We can't fight Calhourn soldiers without help—their numbers are too great.'

'Aren't we closer to Kald? Why shouldn't we go back there and get my people?'

He sighed. He should have known she'd try to fight him on this. 'I mean no offence, but this is a task for Saxon soldiers, not Danes.'

Over the years he had built up an army to protect Braewood and Termarth from possible invasion by the Northmen, and now he was going to use those men to rescue Northmen and the King from Saxons. Everything was all wrong—including his feelings. How could this be happening?

'We're all meant to be on the same side now, aren't we?' she said, sarcasm lacing her voice. But never-theless she seemed to accept his answer. She stood,

not with him, a man who was more male, more virile than any she'd met before.

Her body was still burning in all the places where he had held her in his uncompromising hold earlier. When she'd been encased in his muscled arms, he had been too strong for her. She had been angry and scared at what was being done to her friend, but the tingles he'd sent dancing up and down her spine when he'd smoothed his hands over her back had been equally terrifying. And when he'd tenderly stroked her hair, she had been horrified when she'd almost sunk into him, seeking more of his comfort.

She knew how attraction worked between a man and woman—she'd seen it unfold many times between her people back at home in Kald—but she'd never experienced any of those feelings for herself. She'd meant what she'd told Ash earlier, about not needing a man to complete her. She was happy as she was. Or as happy as she thought she could ever be, given what she had been through. She had decided for herself that she would never marry. She would never feel the same way other men and women did towards each other. She had accepted she would never know that attraction. Until now.

It was no surprise that she felt shaken and confused—first they'd been ambushed, then her friend had been attacked, and now they were tiptoeing around their enemy's camp, trying not to be discovered. But she knew her feelings also had a lot to do with the man at her side, his hands now curling around her calf as he steadied her position.

him in horror. The horse looked strong enough to carry both of them, even Ash's large frame, but that wasn't her concern.

'Why did we just take one horse? Why didn't we take two?' she asked, her throat tight.

He must have seen her startled look, heard the alarm in her voice, and she didn't want to show him she was afraid. But she couldn't help it.

'Because that would have drawn too much attention. They may not notice one go missing, but two... The last thing we need is men on our tail. Come on, Svea. Move up.'

And without warning he suddenly mounted the horse behind her. She let out a strangled protest as his legs straddled hers and his arms came around her. Again.

His large hands gripped hers, firm but gentle, taking the reins from her, and she instantly let go, breaking the connection, letting him take control. So much for standing up to him, she thought. And where was her false bravado when she needed it?

She closed her eyes briefly and blew out a series of breaths, trying to stay calm. She was all too aware of his chest pressing against her back, his thighs tightening around hers as he spurred the horse on, and she tried to make herself as small and as rigid as possible.

'Just relax,' he said.

Relax? How could she possibly relax? She was aware of his every movement, of the taut muscles in his thighs rubbing against her legs, his mighty arms surrounding her, embracing her, and she was con-

ing feelings apart from trying to banish them, block them out as if they didn't exist.

She felt him sigh. 'You're safe with me, Svea. Believe it or not, your boyish looks and fierce mannerisms aren't that tempting!'

'Good!' she raged.

But she felt him grin into her ear, and couldn't decide if he was teasing her or not. She always wanted to be seen as one of the men in Kald—it was what she strived for—and yet, ludicrously, she felt wounded by Ash's comment. Did he not find her attractive? And why did that bother her? It was a good thing, wasn't it?

She forced herself to focus on the dimly lit path ahead, telling herself she could do this. She could do anything to protect her people, even be in close proximity to a Saxon. A dangerously attractive Saxon. She tried to reassure herself that he would have attacked her already if he'd wanted to. He had not once been heavy-handed with her. Instead, he'd saved her life, had shown concern for her safety—had even attempted to patch up her injury. There was no reason to think he would harm her now. He had been careful with her so far. Besides, he didn't even think she was womanly.

She suddenly felt a pang of loss for her mother, and all she could have learnt from her if she'd still been alive. Talking about her earlier must have brought old emotions to the surface. She'd only had her father and brother for guidance, and although she knew she had been lucky to have such a strong bond with

surprise, once the animal had halted, Ash lowered himself down, picking up the reins and leading them through the bracken.

'What are you doing?'

Had she said something wrong? And why was she now missing his warmth? It was absurd.

'Giving you some space. That's what you want, is it not? Now we're a safe distance from the camp we can afford to slow our pace a little. I had the feeling our riding together was making you uncomfortable.'

She felt sure she heard him mutter the words *'and me, too'* under his breath.

'You're right,' he said. 'We should have taken two horses.'

She couldn't understand his conciliatory efforts. Ash wasn't acting like a typical Saxon male, who just took what he wanted where women were concerned. Despite the fact she'd just been getting used to sitting so close to him, to being in his arms, he seemed to be putting her thoughts and feelings before his own and it caught her off guard.

Had she got him all wrong? It made her feel guilty.

'Aren't you tired from walking all day?' she asked.

'I'm used to being on my feet. Don't worry about me... Unless you *want* me to get back up?' he said, looking up at her and flashing her a grin in the moonlight.

She shook her head vehemently. Of course she didn't!

'You don't need to hold the reins, you know. I'm perfectly capable of riding on my own,' she snapped.

in the woods and had come across a man. She'd attacked him as a form of self-defence, only to discover he had been unaware she was even there.

Perhaps she was all the things Ash had said. She made a silent vow to herself now that if they were to survive this, she would try to change.

He halted the horse again and looked up at her, his dark eyes softening. 'You couldn't have done anything to prevent this, Svea. You fought well, and you're doing everything you can to get your men back.' He started walking again. 'If it's any consolation, I feel the same. I keep going over everything in my head. I shouldn't have let my men drink last night, for a start—not when we had a journey ahead—and I shouldn't have allowed you to come with us as our guide.'

She couldn't believe he was admitting that he felt he was to blame. Most men never did that, and she knew from being in his company for just one day that Ash wasn't one to show his emotions. But she liked it that he had. It took a strong man to admit when he was at fault, even if she didn't see that he actually was. He'd done everything he could to fight and protect his men.

'Some guide... I actually don't know where I am now.' She laughed bitterly. 'Do you?'

'Yes, fortunately I know this forest. There's a little grove up ahead. It's sheltered and hard to find, even more so in the dark. We can stop there and rest for the night. I doubt anyone would find us there. We should be safe.'

Normally he would have provided his assistance, but she'd made it very clear he wasn't to touch her, so he'd stayed away. He wondered what had happened to make her shy away from touch. He had the strong desire to rectify it, to show her just how pleasurable it could be, but he knew she wouldn't let him. And he had told her she could trust him.

He'd been pleased when she'd opened up to him, even enjoyed her nervous babbling—until her unintentional words had hit their mark. For hadn't he been pretending to be something he wasn't his whole life? He'd tried to be a child his parents would want. He'd tried to behave the way the monks had wanted him to at the monastery, but it had never been good enough. Now in the service of the King, he had found satisfaction basking in the glow of his monarch's approval, but he knew he was still suppressing a part of him, lying to himself and others. Why did he want to hide that dark side of him so badly? Why did he care so much what people thought? He wished he could be more like Svea in that respect.

'I still don't see why this is necessary,' she pouted as she settled down beneath a large oak, her arms tightly crossed over her chest. It was hard to see anything in the darkness, but by the sound of her voice, she was most displeased with his idea to bed down here for the night.

'You'll feel better for a rest,' he said. 'And try not to worry about our friends. We'll get them back, Svea. I won't let you down.'

He was determined. He would save them, for his

would be in the fields, threshing and ploughing, and the women would be grinding the grains. Yet despite it being his home, the image of Braewood didn't exactly conjure up many memories of comfort or happiness. He'd wanted to stay as a boy, but he'd been sent away. Now as a man, it was hard to feel a connection to the place. He wondered how the people would feel if he did become ruler there, after his father passed. Would they still whisper and cower away from him, as they had when he was a child? Or would he now be able to command their respect? Did he even want to, or would he feel like an imposter, walking the hallways?

He wondered how his father would react to him bringing a Dane through his door. Not well at all, he thought. In fact, he couldn't imagine either he or Svea receiving a warm welcome. His people had hated her kind for years, and they had good reason, but he was starting to see that not all Danes were the same. It gave him hope. He was starting to see her for who she really was—someone who was willing to help others before herself, someone strong yet kind. Could it be possible that one day his people could see her like that, too?

And she was breathtakingly beautiful. He knew his feelings towards her, as a Saxon lord, went against everything his people deemed acceptable. He was expected to marry a respectable Saxon lady. If anyone were to find out he was attracted to a Danish woman, it would not go down well. To many, she was seen as a heathen. And he had to conform, do what was ex-

No one had ever cared to listen about how he felt about things when he'd been growing up. No one had even wanted to talk to him, or share his company. He had often sought solace in the stables in Braewood, making friends with the animals, and then at the monastery, he made it his role to look after the horses they used for transport. It was only when his actions on the battlefield had begun to get him noticed that men had started to ask for his advice and had wanted to be around him and seen at his side. Now the men were keen to serve him and the King requested his frank assessment of situations often, and it was easy to give a point of view on something impartial. He wondered if they would still respect him if they knew the truth about him. He doubted it. But when it came to expressing his own feelings, his hopes and desires... No. It was just something he didn't do. Yet with Svea...there was something about her that made him let down his guard, just a little. Ash wondered if there was a part of him, the unknown part, the part he usually crushed and tried to deny, that was making him attracted to this woman, as if like was being drawn to like?

Svea suddenly threw an arm out in her sleep, her hand coming to land on the side of his chest—and he stilled. If ever he had wanted to test his true character, this was it. His greatest temptation had been put in front of him, just a whisper away, so close he could smell the floral scent of her hair...but he wasn't allowed to go near her. Talk about torture. Yet he was determined he wouldn't be the person his mother and

Chapter Three

When Svea woke, and she realised she was staring into the extraordinary face of Ashford Stanton, her fingers resting against his solid chest—she gasped. Instinct had her snatching back her arm in horror. She had warned him not to come near her, had made it very clear she was not to be touched, and here she was, draped all over him! She was appalled. Thank goodness he was still asleep and would never know.

Sitting up, being careful not to wake him, she raked her hand over her tousled hair and her sleepy face, glad to see the grove now bathed in early-morning sunlight. It was a pretty, tranquil place, and Ash had been right—if anyone had been following them it would have been hard to find them here. He had done well to discover it in the dark.

She stared down at her companion, watching the steady rise and fall of his broad chest, and took the opportunity to openly study his handsome, now familiar face. The harsh angles of his brow and jaw were softened by slumber, and his usually neat tied-back hair

Svea started at his low, deep voice, mortified that she'd been caught staring. 'No!' she spat, turning away and feigning disgust, her cheeks heating. 'You had an insect crawling on your face and I was thinking about swatting it. Hard. That's all.'

He grinned. 'I'm glad you didn't. Did you sleep well?' he asked, sitting up and immediately pulling his hair back into its band. She'd noticed he seemed to be a bit of a perfectionist when it came to his appearance, keen to look neat and tidy. Part of her wished he'd left his hair down...she rather liked the relaxed Ash.

'Not really.'

She didn't know why his smile grew wider. 'Well, tonight you can look forward to a more comfortable bed at Braewood.'

For some reason that thought didn't put her at ease at all. She was so far out of her familiar territory already. Usually it was she and Brand who would host guests, in their humble surroundings at Kald. She prided herself on preparing good food and creating a welcoming environment for the villagers and any travellers in the longhouse. She liked looking after people. She had learnt that from her mother when she was little. She would always help her prepare food for the evening meal. And cooking a feast and looking after guests was a way of keeping her memory alive.

But Svea had never been a guest at someone else's home, let alone a Saxon's fortress. She wasn't sure what to expect, or how she should behave, and she felt a knot tighten in her stomach.

They exited the forest and traversed over rolling

quench his thirst, and then at a few high points which offered teasing glimpses of the sea in the distance. She knew she should be pleased they were nearing their destination, but upon seeing the various landmarks, and hearing Ash talk about his home, her nerves only increased. She was, however, delighted to learn that the fortress was located on the coast. The ocean had always helped to calm her.

The first thing she'd done when she'd been well enough, after she'd been attacked in Termarth as a girl, was go into the sea to wash away the dirt and the shame. She had stayed in there so long, trying to get clean, trying to wash off the stain those men had left on her body, that she hadn't cared about the cold.

Brand had come looking for her, and had finally had to drag her out. He'd wrapped her in furs and sat her by the fire, fussing around her. But she'd done the same again the next day, and a swim in the sea had become her daily source of comfort since. It helped her to feel clean, almost pure again, during the time she was in there, and she also felt closer to her mother, knowing that somewhere she lay deep beneath the surface.

She would need to seek the ocean's strength in Braewood as she wasn't sure how she would be received there. Ash himself had admitted that his people didn't get along with Danes.

'I promise you will be safe and under my protection, Svea,' he said, as if he could sense her apprehension.

Suddenly a thundering noise sent vibrations across

was why she had worked so hard to be one of the best on the battlefield. But, despite her show of strength, it was as if the gods were taunting her, forcing her to relive her attack through memories over and over again. She knew the past few days had heightened her emotions, but she wasn't sure how many more times she could pretend to be all right about it.

'Can't you tell them who you are? That you're a Saxon, too?'

'It's not me I'm worried about! By the colour of your hair, your eyes—hell, even the markings on your skin—they'll know you're a Dane,' he said, sounding almost annoyed with her, his hand coming up to curl over her braids and pull them down over her neck to cover up the dark swirls. 'It will be better for you to be seen as my property, not my ally,' he said, nodding to the makeshift bonds to explain why he'd created them. 'Give me your sword.'

Her hand gripped the hilt firmly. 'No!' It was her mother's sword and her only protection. She prided herself on being able to defend herself or die trying...

'I'm your protection now,' he ground out. 'Please believe I'm doing this for your own good. I don't want to frighten you, Svea, but now is not the time to argue.'

She scowled, gripping the sword even tighter. By the deafening sound of the horses' hooves, and the feel of the ground rumbling beneath her feet, she knew their enemy was almost upon them.

'Svea,' he pressed, leaning in close. 'You're an incredibly beautiful woman and those men... Most of

of their ride. He removed his crested helmet and smoothed down his greasy hair. He reminded her of a peacock. He had a mean, conceited face and his eyes raked over their attire, assessing Ash's Saxon armour and no doubt realising he must be a man of status if he could afford a slave.

'And to you.'

She noticed Ash was careful not to place his hand on the hilt of his sword, not wanting to incite any conflict. He just stood proud, assured. But with the point of view of someone who was beginning to know his behaviour, from spending so much time in his company, she saw the tension visible in his neck and in the rigidity of his stance.

The leader turned his eye to his spear, which he was twirling in his hand, as if the long, sharp weapon somehow proved his manhood. Svea resisted rolling her eyes. She wished she could snatch her sword back from Ash.

'We're looking for a Saxon camp in Alderbury Forest. Have you passed through that way?'

Ash nodded. 'Aye, we saw it. You're heading in the right direction. If you keep going, you'll be sure to come across it.'

The man's eyes narrowed on them. 'Then you must have heard. Calhourn soldiers are rallying men to march on Termarth. The people have had enough of our King making friends with the Danes. Won't you be joining us?'

Svea was suddenly very relieved Ash had had the foresight to discard the tabard that marked his alle-

a bargaining man. But even if I were, I have no silver to pay you. And, as you can see, I'm travelling light.'

'From where I'm standing, it looks like you have all the riches in the world. Especially to me and my men, who have been riding for two days. We could do with some entertainment. Tell you what—just hand over that pretty slave girl of yours, soldier, and we'll allow you to be on your way.'

Svea swallowed. Normally she would have reached for her sword, lashed out by now. But she was beginning to realise she didn't just have herself to think about. If she started a fight she would need Ash's help to finish it. They really were in this together. And Ash had taken her weapon, so she had no choice but to do as she'd been told.

Ash reached for her, his hand clenching roughly around the metal bond he'd created. She gasped.

'What? This thing?' He lifted her wrist as if to show she was his property. 'She belongs to me. She's a good worker—and unfortunately, my lords, she's not for sale.'

The man's lips curled into a sneer. 'Everything has a price. And she's just a heathen, only good for one thing. She's certainly not worth losing your head over.'

Svea staggered forward, livid. 'Give me a sword and I'll dismember you both…' she said scathingly, unable to help herself. So much for trying to change.

'Quiet!' both Ash and the brute barked in unison.

'The girl is mine,' Ash said. 'If you want her, you'll

haps...perhaps you should hand me over,' she said, her mouth dry.

It was her absolute worst fear, but she would sacrifice herself to save her men if she had to. And she knew she needed Ash alive to do that.

He looked at her as if she had gone mad. He took a step towards her and stroked a finger down her cheek. 'Never.'

She swallowed. 'You need to get home, raise the *fyrd*. Think of the King. You said so yourself—we're his only hope. If something should happen to you...'

His dark face rarely gave anything away. And yet by the crease in his heavy brow she could tell that he was angry—with her, for suggesting he give her up, and with these men.

'Then I will have died fighting for a worthy cause,' he said, his eyes levelling with hers. 'And I will meet my death with honour, should it come to that. But, Svea, if something happens to me I want you to run. Run fast into those trees over there. Find somewhere to hide. Just don't look back,' he whispered. 'Promise me you will do that?'

She nodded, numb, tears threatening. She hardly ever cried—and especially not in front of men. She didn't know what the matter was with her. She just knew she needed him to win. To stay alive.

When Ash turned around the man was ready for him, and immediately—unfairly—struck the first blow. His blade sliced through Ash's chin, and Svea gasped in shock at seeing his blood. Another scar to add to his many others...

never seen such a skilled warrior. In any other fight he would have been spectacular to watch, but as her destiny was entwined with every slice of that sword, this one was unbearable. She almost turned her face into the horse's flank, but knew she must see every moment of this fight.

The slashings and stabbings became quicker and more ferocious, and when the peacock's blade sliced through Ash's waist Svea gasped. But incredibly Ash carried on, as if he hadn't felt a thing, bearing down on the stranger. Svea and the men on horseback watched in awe. She could tell both men were tiring now, under their heavy chainmail and weapons, but Ash seemed to be drawing on a last reserve of strength, and with one final, brutal blow he knocked the weapon out of his opponent's hand and the man fell, scurrying backwards, his face forlorn.

Reining in their agitated horses, the Saxon riders looked on in mute horror as their leader surely faced imminent death. Svea's heart lifted just a little. After the words he'd threatened her with, she wouldn't be sorry.

In a desperate last-ditch attempt to regain his blade, the peacock crawled along the ground—but Ash was swift, conclusive. He pinned the man to the floor, his boot on his chest and the tip of his sword to the brute's chin.

'Who *are* you?' the peacock asked.

'I am Lord Stanton of Braewood.'

A hushed gasp rippled around the group. The man gulped against the sharp blade. 'Lord Stanton... I did not know it was you.'

do what they liked, take what they wanted, without suffering the consequences?

He knew many Saxon men who thought they could do what they desired to Danish women. They saw it as their right, and it disgusted him. Especially now he was beginning to respect and admire Svea for all that she was.

He had fought bloody and hard, and his muscles were weary—but he'd do it all again if he had to.

'Are you all right?' he asked, turning to Svea while wiping his brow with the back of his hand.

When he'd seen those men approach, all he'd thought about was keeping her safe. And when Elrick had leered at her he'd seen a look of pure dread pass across her features. He'd hated to see her so vulnerable, and again he had scolded himself for his foolishness for letting her leave Kald in the first place. When the man had said he would be her new master, he'd wanted to run him through. The thought of any man laying his hands on her was too much to bear.

'Me? Yes.' She nodded, her lip trembling. 'You?'

He pressed a hand to his chin. 'I'll mend.'

But as he crossed the distance between them his lower abdomen burned with pain and he winced. He hadn't noticed it before…

'You're hurt. Is it bad? Let me see.'

'It's nothing. I've had worse.'

'Let me look. Sit down. Over there,' she said, motioning to a low part in the field wall.

He shook off his heavy chainmail to reveal a dark stain spreading across his tunic, and cursed. Svea

'And I think you still resent me for stopping you from taking revenge on Lord Crowe.'

'That doesn't mean I want you dead.'

'Thank goodness. I don't think I'd stand a chance against that sword of yours. Which reminds me—here,' he said. And he pulled her blade from his scabbard, handing it back to her.

Her face relaxed and she smiled in pure relief. He smiled back as they locked eyes with each other for a moment.

'This is my mother's sword.'

'It's very beautiful.' He didn't break eye contact.

'I could have taken him myself, you know.'

'I know.' He shrugged.

She poured some of the water onto a corner of his cloak. Then she lifted his tunic again and tentatively began to wipe the blood away from his wound with the damp material. There was a slight tremble in her fingers. He blanched.

'This might sting for a moment,' she said, biting her lip. 'Sorry.'

She dabbed gently at the wound, doing the best she could. He leaned back a little, to give her better access. She was so close he could smell rose petals again.

'You know, you could have just handed me over to save your own skin…to protect the King. Why didn't you?'

'Perhaps for the same reason I saved you on the battlefield instead of the King. Instinct.'

She sat back on her knees, halting in what she was doing. 'I thought that was merely circumstance.'

And just how much trouble could he cause from his sickbed?

'The way you fight… You remind me of a Dane. How is it that you are not afraid of anything?'

He studied her. Was that what she thought? If only she knew the truth. That deep down he was afraid of who he was, and of what other people would think of him if they discovered the truth. It was something that had haunted him his entire life—the thought of the damage his secret could do to his honour if word got out. He feared that he was monstrous—although every moment he spent with Svea helped to confirm to him that not all Danes were like that. It was good for him. *She* was good for him.

'Actually, I am,' he said. 'I'm afraid of the rain.'

'The rain?' she asked.

'Yes,' he said, shaking his still-loose hair. 'Because it makes my hair curl.' He gave a mock shudder.

She stared at him, incredulous. And then she let out a laugh—and it was the most delightful sound he'd ever heard.

'I can't believe that you, of all people, are making a joke at a time like this.'

'Me "of all people"?' he asked, his eyebrow raised quizzically.

She shrugged. 'I confess I thought you were boring. Haughty. I did not know you had a sense of humour.'

'I hide it well.' *As with other things*, he thought. 'Now *your* hair… It's blonder than when I saw you

that she might tense and cast him off at any moment. Skating his fingers gently up and under her sleeve, he pushed it backwards, making her shiver under his touch, and he revealed more dark swirling patterns on her skin there.

'And this one? What does it say?'

'This is the Helm of Awe. It offers protection against the abuse of power. It also helps to curb my fear.'

His smile slipped. 'Did someone hurt you, Svea?' He continued to hold her.

'A long time ago, yes. I had a bad experience.'

His thumb smoothed over her delicate skin. 'What kind of bad experience?'

She looked up into his eyes. 'The worst kind.'

His heart crumbled for her. His stomach churned.

With his other hand he reached out to touch her cheek lightly, reverently. 'Was it Crowe?'

'Yes.'

He cursed under his breath, felt a sudden spurt of rage shafting through his body. 'You're right. I should have let you kill him when you had the chance.'

For an instant she looked shocked that he was conceding she'd been right, and then suddenly she came up on her knees and kissed him. It was a soft, gentle kiss on the cheek, and so spontaneous it took them both by surprise. It was as if she was thanking him for finally agreeing with her. For being on her side. For understanding.

And then, just as quickly as she'd done it, she bowed her head, flustered, as if she was as disturbed

Chapter Four

They'd been passing teasing glimpses of the sea through the trees for a while when finally, underneath a large grey storm cloud, the three blackened turrets of Braewood Keep came into view. Ash grimaced. He had always thought the building said a lot about who he was. It served as a stark reminder of an attack that had left its mark on the fortified tower, never to be forgotten. He saw the flawed keep as a reflection of himself...commanding, one of the country's greatest strongholds, yet scarred, damaged by the past. And no one had ever cared enough to restore it to its original condition.

Svea had insisted on him riding, due to his injuries, but he had refused, until finally she had agreed to share the horse with him to speed up their journey. And this time she hadn't held herself so stiffly away from him, but had allowed him to pull her back into his chest, letting him hold her. And strangely, despite the pouring rain and their sodden clothes, now they

impenetrable imposing wall, in case the Northmen should ever return.

As they drew closer Ash noticed a commotion going on outside the main gate. There seemed to be people strewn about, sitting in little self-made shelters erected against the stone walls, shivering in the rain, trying to keep feeble fires going.

'What is this now?' he muttered.

Suddenly he felt weary. They'd had a long trip across the countryside and the rain hadn't ceased all morning. They were soaked through and cold, and he wanted to get Svea in front of a fire with a hot meal as soon as possible.

He slowed the horse as they approached the throng of people, and resisted putting his hand to the hilt of his sword.

'Lord Stanton,' the gatekeeper said, recognising him and rushing forward. 'Welcome home.'

'What's going on here?'

'They're Danes, my lord. All of them. Every day more of them arrive, seeking shelter after their settlements have been attacked.'

He felt Svea tense at the man's words.

'They say they only wish to help tend our lands in return for shelter and food, but your father refuses to let them in, my lord. Yet still they will not leave, saying they have nowhere to go. Some are sick or wounded—and many have young children. But Braewood soldiers have been forbidden from helping them.'

Ash nodded, and took a moment to assess the situ-

And as the settlers began to tentatively stumble through the gates, hesitantly handing over their blades or arrows, he spoke to them once more.

'You have my word that you will be safe here, under my protection. And we shall find work for you on the land if you wish to earn your keep. I shall send food and water imminently.'

Ash was furious with his father. He had always been willing to give up his lands, his position here, thinking it the best for his people, but he was starting to wonder if that was the case. Looking around him, he wondered if his father and his outdated thinking was doing more damage than good. And the thought of having another sparring match with the man made Ash feel jaded.

He wondered what Svea was making of all this. It wasn't exactly a good first impression.

The thought surprised him. Did he want her to like it here?

Murmurs of appreciation and thanks rumbled through the people as he and Svea helped them move their few belongings. Ash picked up a small child who was crying and carried the boy inside the safety of the fortress walls, while Svea tended to the wounds of those who had been injured. Once a fire had been lit the people seemed in better spirits, and Ash saw an opportunity to pull Svea to one side, tugging her arm to follow him.

'You did well out here. Thank you,' he said. He tipped his head in the direction of the hall. 'Come on. I'll show you around…get you settled in.'

She had to admit she was curious to see the inside of Ash's home, to try to understand him better. Outside, it was even grander than she could have imagined. The stone fortifications were so high and forbidding she doubted any enemy would ever get through or over them. And yet the tall tower of the keep, which rose up into the rain clouds, was rather ominous—especially with just three remaining crumbling turrets, which seemed to have been ravaged by an old fire.

Stepping inside, she saw there was a fire burning in a large hall which wasn't too dissimilar from the longhouse in Kald, with benches and animal skins and furs scattered about. It was cosy and inviting— or was it the heat radiating from Ash's hand holding hers that was making her feel warm? It was as if she could feel every contradictory rough and smooth part of the long, large fingers steadily holding hers, offering her reassurance. But as a portly lady jostled towards them, giving Ash a warm smile, he discreetly released her from his grip. She immediately missed the contact.

'My lord, you're home! What a pleasant surprise. Good heavens—just look at the state of you! Are you hurt? What has happened?'

'We've had a long and somewhat eventful journey, Ellette. This is Svea, a friend from Kald.'

Svea and Ellette acknowledged each other with a little nod, and the woman's eyes swept over her wet warrior's attire. Svea had the feeling this woman didn't miss a thing.

Ellette led her up the stairs to a narrow corridor and opened a little door at the end. Svea took in the large room before her. It was very grand compared to her simple farmstead back in Kald. There was a large bed in the middle, covered in various furs, and there was a small table and a barrel to bathe in. She stood awkwardly by the door as Ellette helped a servant to fill it, bringing bucket after bucket of steaming hot water. She tried to offer her assistance, but Ellette batted her away.

When the door was finally shut on her, and she was alone for the first time in days, she just stood there, taking it all in. The bed looked comfortable and inviting, and she longed to sink down onto it, to rest her weary body, but she didn't want to get it damp from her wet clothes, so she quickly untied her braids and removed her dirty, sodden garments, dropping them to the floor.

Tentatively, she stepped into the barrel. At home in Kald she was quite happy bathing in the sea, with the icy surf invigorating her body, but this was a whole new experience. Sinking under the surface, she let the warm water lap against her skin. It felt wonderful, and helped to soothe her tired and aching muscles.

She tipped her head back, allowing the water to soak into her hair, to ripple across her face and clean away the mud and the rain. She wondered if somewhere in this fortress Ash, too, was washing off the blood and grime from their journey. She hoped his wound was all right. It hadn't looked too deep...she thought it just needed to be kept clean.

her fingers slowly downwards to reach between her legs, where she was experiencing flickers of excitement when she thought of him. She tentatively ran her fingers through her neat curls and below, parting the intimate folds of her skin.

She thought of Ash's large hands stroking over her shoulder, running through her hair, and she began to probe, pressing her finger against the tiny nub that was screaming out to be touched. Her head tipped back as she circled it, opening herself up with wider, firmer movements, delighting in the incredible sensations she was creating, in this wonderful newfound pleasure rocking through her body. She spread her legs wider, moved her fingers faster, thinking of his thighs pressing against hers, her bottom shifting against his groin, his dark brown gaze watching her...

A knock on the door brought her to her senses.

She sat bolt upright in the barrel, shocked. *What on earth was she doing?*

Her cheeks hot, her heart pounding, she wiped the water out of her face. 'Yes?' she choked.

'It's just me, love.' It was Ellette. 'I have some clean clothes for you. Can I come in?'

Svea tucked her knees to her chest, trying to cover herself. She wasn't used to anyone seeing her without clothes on. She had always been a private person. She only ever bathed in the sea in Kald when she was sure no one else was around.

'All right.'

The kindly woman stepped through the door and

she drew the silky material together at her waist with the gold-laced braid and studied herself again in the shiny metal circle.

She would never usually wear anything that would draw attention to her cleavage, or her waist. She'd had to for the wedding, because Anne had requested it, and Brand had begged her to wear a pretty dress to please his bride, but that had been once only. She usually hid her figure under masculine clothes. She usually made her own garments—badly.

She smoothed down the silk skirt, feeling nervous. What would Ash think of her wearing this? Why did she care?

She was curiously apprehensive as she slowly made her way back down the spiral staircase, wondering what she would find in the hall. Her nerves were as tightly wound as the steps. Was it to be just her and Ash having dinner together? Or would the people from the settlement be there? That was what happened at home in Kald. Everyone piled into the longhouse for the evening meal, catching up on the news of the day, sharing stories. In comparison, it was very quiet here.

But as her foot hit the bottom stair she heard raised voices. She halted, straining to listen. It was Ash, and another deep voice she didn't recognise. She pulled back a few steps, hiding herself from view.

'Well, she's no longer here, is she? She doesn't decide!' Ash barked, before slamming the door on whoever he was arguing with and striding out into the corridor. She watched as he smoothed a hand over

cheeks flushed at the erotic thought. She had never wished for such a thing to happen before. What was he doing to her? He was making her long for things that surely could never be.

Usually she'd do something to make herself look less attractive, or to detract attention from herself, but she didn't think she could even move. He looked rakishly good-looking. His dark hair had been tamed into a neat knot again, and he'd trimmed his beard back to a shorter style. It was the first time she'd seen him without his armour, in normal clean clothes, and the way his tunic clung to his sculpted body was mesmerising. Magnetic. Her mouth dried.

He rose to meet her, stepped towards her. 'Svea, you look…'

'Like a girl?' she said, preventing him from giving her a compliment.

'You took the words right out of my mouth!' He grinned wolfishly.

'Yes, well, I usually wear a tunic. I'm not used to such fine clothes.'

'You wear them well.'

He looked her up and down again, and she was surprised to find she didn't mind. Normally she'd do anything to avoid a man's scrutiny.

'Very well.'

His eyes were proprietorial, and she realised she liked it. His words from before floated through her mind. *'The girl is mine.'*

'Whose are they?' she croaked.

'They were my mother's.'

'If a little unwelcoming? Go on—you can say it.' He grimaced.

'No, Ellette has been lovely. Too kind, really. But the place seems rather empty.' She suddenly felt a pang for her home, her friends. Ash's stronghold was huge, and yet most of the people were outside rather than inside. It seemed hollow, somehow, as if it was a body missing its beating heart.

'It's always been that way,' he said.

'Do you not wish to change it?'

When he frowned, she wished she'd been more careful with her words.

'That's up to my father. Despite his illness, he's still in charge.'

'You were the one making decisions today...'

'Which I may come to regret.'

'You couldn't leave those people to die out there in the cold. Winter is on its way. They were starving, hurt... You did the right thing, Ash.'

'My father is most displeased that I went against his orders.'

So it *was* his father he'd been arguing with.

When Ellette came to remove their plates Svea tried to help her, standing to gather their dishes. She wasn't used to having someone wait on her.

Ash gave her a bemused smile.

'It's all right, love, I can do it,' Ellette said. 'You sit down.'

'I'm intrigued...' Ash smirked. 'Are you going to wipe your mouth on your sleeve now? Or were you acting out just for me?'

stomach another blackberry for the rest of her life. Or at least this season!

Ash relaxed back in his chair, smiling at her. And she smiled back warmly. He was such a handsome man, and he had treated her kindly. She was ashamed of the way she'd spoken to him that night at the wedding…especially now he'd saved her life—twice. Just a few days ago he had been her sworn enemy, and now they were sharing jokes…

The thought had her straightening, and she reached over for her cup to take a sobering sip of water. She felt guilty for laughing while her friends were suffering, and for enjoying Ash's company so much.

'I've asked Ellette to look after you while I'm gone,' he said, coming forward to lean on his elbows, suddenly serious, too.

'Gone?' All humour left her.

'I need to ride out to the neighbouring burhs. Each has promised to provide men when the King or Braewood is in need. We won't be helped by the fact that those men we met on the road passed through here on their way from Rainhill—my father fed them and agreed to send men to assist Crowe.'

Svea gasped. 'The men who tried to kill you?'

His lips narrowed. 'Yes. My father and I have had words. I will not let Braewood be associated with those who are an opposing force to the Crown—or the Danes.'

Hope soared inside her. And she realised, despite what he'd said about it being his father's home, not his, that he did care about Braewood and its reputation.

He softened his voice. 'Besides, I'll feel better knowing you're safe here.' He came around the table towards her and took her hand. 'And as for wanting you with me…I think by now you know that I do…'

Her throat felt thick with emotion. She couldn't talk.

He reached out to take her chin between his fingers. 'I'll be back tomorrow. By nightfall, hopefully.'

'You haven't even had a chance to rest your wound…' she whispered.

He leaned in and planted a gentle kiss on her forehead, trailing a hand down her spine, sending tingles dancing after it.

'Don't worry about me, Svea.'

But the trouble was, she did.

After seeing Ash and his men off on their journey, Svea decided she couldn't spend the rest of the day dispirited, wishing he'd allowed her to go with him, wishing she'd ignored his orders and followed him anyway.

She was intrigued to see the ocean in Braewood, so she pulled on his cloak, which had finally dried out by the fire, and made her way down the steep escarpment to the sand beneath. The cloak smelled of him…musky, woody…and she felt a pang in her chest. She had spent so much time in his company it felt odd not to be with him.

Braewood was a beautiful place, the fort having been built into the top of a cliff. The beach was more vast, more wild than the sheltered bay in Kald, and

on things. Although she enjoyed her life in Kald, she was beginning to believe she could be happier. And perhaps she had a right to be.

She walked the length and breadth of the beach, paddling in the icy water tumbling onto the shore, admiring the different rock formations, the grasses and seaweed. She was hunting for pretty shells, thinking she might take them home as a reminder of this magnificent place, when in the clay-like wet sand she came across a small pointed item. She crouched down, washing it off in the salty surf, uncaring that the bottom of her skirts was getting wet, and studied it.

It looked like a tooth. The tooth of a sea dog— those great beasts with dark black fins that rose out of the water. These teeth were a symbol of protection amongst her people, and she knew it was quite a find. She tucked it into the trim of her dress, deciding she would perhaps make it into a necklace and give it to Ash when he returned. If anyone deserved protection it was him. He had earned it.

Svea wondered what it was that kept him from this beautiful place. He had said he didn't get on with his father, but was that the whole truth of it? When they'd arrived, he'd turned heads in the fortress square. The people—both Saxons and Danes—had clearly respected him. What was holding him back from taking up his position here? It was an impressive place, almost as grand as the King's castle in Termarth, and it offered a glimpse of Ash's power to come.

She thought of her daily life back in Kald—how she swept the floors, looked after the livestock and

riosity had been piqued, and the more she roamed, the more she realised she was hoping to learn more about the man she was beginning to have feelings for.

When she entered a small library, she came upon scroll after scroll of diary entries. It was at times like this she wished she could read. Instead, she studied the bejewelled covers, and the pictures inside, tracing her fingers over the drawings on the delicate parchment. She recognised Braewood fort, although in the images there were four turrets, not three, and there were drawings of a beautiful woman—Lady Stanton, perhaps?

But as she turned the pages the images became darker. Fires. Warriors attacking people. Warriors with markings on their skin and boats that looked like longships. Bodies stacked up everywhere, images of death...

She slammed the pages shut, her blood running cold. Had Danes attacked Braewood fortress? It would explain why the building was damaged, and why her kind weren't welcome here. She cast her mind back to what Ash had told her in the forest, about Danes ransacking settlements. Had he witnessed such atrocities first-hand? Had he been hurt? If so, did he blame her? And why hadn't he said anything? He must despise her people. And yet he had stood up for her against those men earlier...

Needing answers, Svea picked up her wet skirts and went to look for Ellette in the back room of the hall.

'I was hoping to be of some use to you,' Svea said

'How so?' Svea dunked the chopped pieces of swede in a large pot and set about peeling another.

'Well, I don't know all the facts, but his parents sent him off to a monastery when he was just a boy. They said he was too feral. They had a strained relationship from the start. He was always different—bigger, stronger than the rest of the boys—and he wanted far too much freedom. He used to roam about the shoreline all day long, and they wanted to tame the wildness out of him. But he was only eight when he left this place…just a child.'

Svea felt a dart of sympathy shoot through her for that little boy. She tried to picture him, with dark hair that curled up at the ends which he just couldn't tame, sad and serious brown eyes… She had lost her mother around that age and it had devastated her. But she'd been able to lean on her father and brother for love and support. Whereas Ash—had he had no one? Her heart went out to him. She wondered what harm such early isolation might have done to him.

'He came back years later, so handsome and very refined. But he was sullen…rather stifled, if you ask me,' Ellette continued.

That would explain a lot, Svea thought. Why he was so reserved at times.

'But between you and me, his father still couldn't love him. It was all such a shame. So he left again—went off out into the world to make his own way. He worked without their support and look at him now—prominent and influential. A favourite of the King.'

Svea thought back to her judgement of him that

riage herself. But the thought of Ash entwining his fingers with another woman's, placing a soft kiss to her forehead, was not a pleasant one.

'But the young Lord has refused. They say his father will not die until he agrees! They're both very stubborn.'

Svea felt a slight trickle of relief at the woman's words. She knew Ash was determined, and he had told her himself he didn't want to marry, but now she wondered why. Was it just to spite his father? Was that the reason?

'Lord Stanton hasn't even tried to bend to his will,' Ellette continued, lowering her voice to hushed tones. 'We all hope he does, of course. It would be wonderful to have a lady to look after the place again. And the young Lord would be a good leader—just look at how he dealt with those people outside.'

Ash had made sure the Danish settlers had all they needed before he'd left, and Svea was glad he'd stuck to his word. She'd come to realise he was not the man she had first thought—he was so much more.

'Was there a fire here once, Ellette? I was wondering what had happened to the keep…to the turrets.'

'Oh, yes, but that was before my time, dear. There was an attack by—'

'Danes?'

'Yes, dear. They arrived on the beach unexpectedly and attacked the settlement here. They were savage—they destroyed everything in their path, or so I've been told. But that was before the young Lord Stanton's time, when his father had just taken

them to help. And then she wondered if any Saxon maidens would be at those settlements.

A vision of a hall full of pretty women, all delicate and lovely, smiling at the handsome lord, filled her mind and she tossed and turned in the bed. She tried to tell herself that Ash knew if they were to have any chance of rescuing the King, and her friends, that he had to act swiftly, so he probably wouldn't have time for any pleasantries... Besides, he'd told her he didn't want to marry or have children. But did that mean he didn't enjoy the casual company of women? She knew how promiscuous the men and women in Kald could be...

No, she could not bear to think about it!

Trying to think of something less disturbing, she wondered what the real reason was that Ash didn't want to rule here. She made up her mind to ask him when he returned, and to learn more about him—if he'd share more with her. And, in turn, she would have to share more with him. Was she ready to talk about her past? She thought perhaps she finally was.

Although Svea tried to keep herself busy, the next day dragged excruciatingly slowly as she waited for any sign of Ash and his men. She helped in the fields for a while, much to Ellette's disapproval, and checked on the people in the barns, whom Lord Aethelbard had thankfully left alone. She went for another long walk on the beach. She fetched eggs and milked some of the cows, and she played with the Danish and Saxon children in the square.

As the day began to fall away she even tried to

Chapter Five

When Ash returned he found Svea curled up, asleep by the fire. Her beautiful blonde locks fell gently across her cheek and he drew them back tenderly, so he could see her face. His heart ached. He'd only been gone a night and a day, but he'd missed her. And he'd raced home as fast as he could just to get back to her, encouraging his men with promises of extra mead and food for their families.

It had made him begin to wonder what it would be like to have her waiting at home for him always… it would certainly make Braewood a more attractive place to settle down. And yet he knew that was a fantasy, and it could never be.

He crouched down and gently touched her shoulder to wake her. 'Svea.'

She stirred but didn't wake, and he took the chance to trace his finger over the dark lines on her neck, learning their pathways. The intricate knotwork fascinated him. *She* fascinated him.

respected lords of their lands and fierce fighters. They've promised at least thirty men each.'

Svea nodded. 'Ellette mentioned Earlington earlier. She said you had a…connection there.'

Ash's eyes narrowed at her tone, at the uncertainty in her eyes. He knew Ellette's mouth had a tendency to run away with her. Had she been talking to Svea about Lady Edith and his father's hopes for Ash to wed her? Was Svea jealous?

His lips curled upwards. 'Just because my father wants something to happen, it doesn't mean it will. I missed you while I was gone.' He trailed a finger down her cheek. 'I have brought you something…'

She sat up straighter.

From behind his back, where he'd placed it on the floor, he pulled out a long-stemmed flower. Huge, bright and yellow, it looked like the sun.

Svea's face beamed as she gingerly took the stem from him. 'It's beautiful! I have never seen anything so joyous before.'

'I know. I saw it and thought of you. You can eat the seeds, too, as I know you're always hungry.'

'Thank you,' she said, laughing.

'Are you hungry now?' he asked. 'I'm starving.'

She nodded.

'Come on, then.'

He gripped her hand in his, entwining his fingers with hers, pleased when she let him, and led her through the hall and down the corridor to the larder. It was late, so most of the settlement's people had re-

His brow furrowed and he put down the remainder of his slice of bread. 'And?'

'Well, I can't read, so the words didn't mean anything to me, but the pictures...'

She stared at him, with questions in her brilliant blue eyes. But he didn't want to talk about it—not now. Just for one night, he didn't want to be reminded of who he was. He didn't want to talk about the past. He didn't want anything to dampen his good mood at being with her again.

'He's very creative, my father,' he said dismissively. 'We should find you a blank book. You could draw some of your designs in there. I'd like to see them. Do you like the beach?'

'I love it. It's so beautiful. I don't know how you can bear to be away from this place.'

Usually it was easy to stay away. But not with Svea here.

'Did Ellette look after you like I asked her to?'

'Very well. And, don't be cross with her, I persuaded her to let me help with some of the household tasks. I did a bit of work in the fields, and with the animals. I also helped with the cooking. I needed something to take my mind off things.'

He wondered if those 'things' had included him. He knew he had barely thought of anything but her while he'd been gone. She never ceased to amaze him. This was meant to be her chance to relax and recuperate after their journey, but instead she'd helped his people, worked on the land and in the kitchen.

'What did you make?'

He moved after her and she tried to make a run for it. But he was too quick, and he grabbed her round the waist and deposited the flour in her hair. She gasped, and then both of them fell about laughing.

'What on earth is going on here?'

The stern voice came from the doorway. They both glanced up to see Ellette in her nightgown, holding an oil lamp, looking vexed.

'I'm so sorry, Ellette. We'll clean it up, I promise,' Svea said, straightening.

'Yes. Make sure you do! And don't wake Lord Aethelbald…there'll be hell to pay,' the woman said, turning on her heel.

Svea bit her lip, trying not to let out another giggle.

'We'd better clean ourselves up first,' Ash said, still laughing, unconcerned about Ellette and her wary gaze. He probably should care about what people thought of his bond with Svea, but surprisingly he didn't. 'Come with me.'

Taking her arm, he tugged Svea through a door and out to the back of the settlement. His fingers strayed down her skin to take her hand in his again, and they walked down the steep path towards the moonlit beach.

'So, what do you think?' he asked, giving her a playful nudge.

'Of what?'

He pointed to the sea. 'A late-night swim.'

'What?' She laughed nervously.

'You *can* swim, can't you?' he asked, goading her.

'Of course I can,' she said. 'Actually, I've wanted

'Then turn around,' she said, and he grinned.

He had known she wasn't one to shirk a challenge.

So he did as he was told, even though they were cloaked in the late-night darkness, so he could barely see her anyway. He listened as she tussled with her gown, and then heard it drop to the sand. The response in his groin was instant. *Damn.* What he wouldn't give to turn around, stride over to her and take her bare body in his arms. But he knew he mustn't. He had said it was to be 'just a swim' and he would stick to his word.

He knew he had to take this slowly. He couldn't be sure what Crowe had done, or just how badly it had affected her. It made him feel sick, just thinking about that man laying his hands on her. He guessed he had caused her some serious damage, given the way she held herself, the way she behaved, and he needed to build her trust—especially where her body was concerned.

'Ready,' she said, stalking past him and running into the water.

The material of his tunic barely reached the top of her thighs, and the sight made him harder. He followed her, laughing. The thought dawned on him that he would follow her anywhere. When he was with her he felt lighter, warmer, as if all the burdens that lay heavy on his mind had abandoned him, or become less somehow. She filled a void in his life and fulfilled his need for fun and friendship. Of course he knew it was much more than that. But to someone who'd never had it, fun and friendship would do for now.

you're saying. I used to come to the sea after an argument with my father, to wash all my worries away.'

Suddenly serious, Svea reached out and touched his arm. Her fingers were cool against his skin. 'Why don't you get on with your father, Ash? Ellette said he was cruel to you, when you were growing up.'

His brows knitted together. 'He did his best.'

She stared at him, removing her fingers and placing her hands on her hips.

'What?' he said, and shrugged.

'Is that all you have to say? All you're going to tell me?' She shook her head at him, frustrated.

He wiped the water out of his eyes, drawing a hand over his face. He didn't want to talk about it. It would ruin the mood. He didn't want to burden her with sob stories from his past. He didn't want to tell her why he didn't get on with his father because he didn't want to share that with anyone. Especially her.

'There's not much to say.'

He wanted to change the subject to something safer. Something less personal. He didn't want to revisit the past. Not tonight.

'But that's not true, is it?' she bit out. 'You fire questions at me all the time, Ash—about my family, my beliefs, where I come from. You're always delving deeper, wanting to know more. But you don't offer me the same courtesy. I ask you questions and you tell me nothing of yourself. How am I supposed to know who you are?'

Hope bloomed inside him at the fact that she wanted to know him. And yet at the same time a pain

He caught up with her on the beach, followed her as she stalked up the sand, the wet tunic clinging to her skin, water dripping down her pale thighs. He tugged her arm to pull her round to face him. 'Svea, wait.'

'I've told you so much about myself, Ash. Don't you think I deserve to know something about you?'

'All right,' he said, his hands on his hips, shaking his wet hair. 'What is it that you want to know?'

'Anything! Everything,' she said. 'I want to know what happened here. What happened to make the turrets of the keep blackened by fire? Why are the walls built so ridiculously high? Why don't you get on with your father? Why did he send you away when you were younger?' She sighed, pausing for breath. 'I want to know why you live in Termarth, and not here. And what are your plans—what are your hopes for the future?'

'Is that all?' he asked sarcastically. He raked his hand through his hair, expressing his annoyance.

'No! I have lots more questions… What are you planning to do when all this is over? Will you be going back to Termarth once you rescue the King?'

'I doubt he'll have me.' He laughed bitterly.

'What do you mean?'

'I swore an oath to protect him and I let him down…'

'You didn't. You haven't. Not yet.'

'I did, Svea,' he said, taking a step towards her. 'Because it wasn't the King I was driven by desire to protect. If it had been, *he* might be standing here with me now—not you.'

at the thrilling and tender feelings rushing through her body.

Her knees buckled, she began to sway, and he caught her with his arm, hauling her closer. As his silky hot tongue delved deeper, rolling over her like the ocean waves, drawing her in, pulling her under, sending searing heat charging through her, she curled her toes into the sand. His other hand trailed down to brush over the sensitive skin on her neck. His thumb was at her throat, circling her pulse, and an insane need lanced her.

She had never imagined a kiss could feel so good, sending signals to every part of her body, telling her she wanted more. And it was as if Ash could read her mind, because his hand drifted down to cup one full, heavy breast in his palm and she moaned. She'd thought she'd never allow a man to touch her again, but as he gently kneaded, softly squeezing her flesh with his fingers, pressing his thumb lightly against her pebble-hard nipple through the wet material, she welcomed the sensations he was creating. And as he twisted and teased the hard peak, his lips still ravaging her mouth, a low moan escaped from her throat and her head tipped backwards.

He took a moment to stray from her mouth, his lips roaming down her neck, kissing and licking, tormenting her with his clever tongue, moving to the base of her ear, all the time whispering how beautiful she was. Excitement pooled between her legs. Then he came back to her lips again, claiming her mouth once more.

Her face flushed, her hair dishevelled, she couldn't bring herself to look at him. She felt so ashamed. Instead, she grabbed up her dress from the sand and ran.

tion. And she'd seemed to come alive under his touch. She'd pressed herself against him as if she wanted him, squirmed against him as if she needed satisfaction… And he'd wanted to give it to her. He'd never wanted anything so much.

'Svea, you're going to have to face me eventually. Can you please open the door?'

He pressed his ear against the wood and heard gentle footsteps behind the door, as if she were pacing up and down. He softened his voice. 'You can't just bury your head in the Braewood sand and pretend it never happened. You can't hide from me forever. Come on…you know I'm right…'

Finally he heard her pad over to the door, and slowly she opened it a little. He took in her wide blue eyes, her flushed cheeks, her lip caught between her teeth. Thank goodness she'd had the sense to change into dry clothes—a long white nightgown Ellette must have given her. She looked stunning, with her damp long blonde hair tumbling down over her shoulders. This virginal vision of her didn't help to ease his desire, but at least she was wearing more material than before. He swallowed. More material was good. He didn't know if he'd have had the strength to stay away from her if she'd still been standing there in that clinging wet tunic.

He, too, had had the sense to pull on a dry tunic and breeches before coming up here, although his feet were bare and he hadn't warmed up yet. But that probably had more to do with her cool treatment of him rather than their late-night swim.

He crouched down before her, so their eyes were level. He was starting to think this was more to do with the 'bad experience' she'd mentioned on their journey from Kald rather than with him. But unless she told him the full story he couldn't help her.

'Svea, do you want to tell me about it? About what happened with Lord Crowe.'

She shook her head, cringing at hearing the man's name.

He reached out to take her cheek in his palm, bringing her eyes back to his. 'It might help.'

Tears welled in her eyes and she wrung her hands. She opened her mouth to speak but no words came out. She swallowed and tried again. 'I've never told anyone about it before...' she managed, her voice wavering. 'My brother told our people in Kald, after it happened. But I find it hard to speak about it. It's too painful.'

'I know all about pain. And I know it's hard to talk about bad things that have happened in the past. Why do you think I say so little?'

She gave him a sad smile. 'You have bad memories that consume you, too?'

'Yes. And I know it hurts to remember... But perhaps, if you share them, I can help?'

She nodded. 'I want to try. And I know that you deserve to hear the truth, Ash. Perhaps, if I tell you, it will help to explain why I behaved as I did out there on the beach. Maybe you'll forgive me.'

She took a deep breath and he realised she was about to begin—to tell him her story. He thought how

'Brand and I were reeling from what had happened, just standing there, trying to comprehend what they'd done. Through the shock and the pain, I think we realised we might be next, so we tried to make a run for it. Brand managed to get away, and I was glad, but I wasn't so lucky. The men grabbed me. The leader—Crowe—ripped at my clothes, and while his men held me down he raped me. When he'd finished, he let them take turns with me. I had just turned twelve.'

Ash squeezed his eyes shut, trying to fight the horrific images flooding his mind. He dragged a hand over his face. His heart went out to her for what she'd gone through, what she'd suffered. It was horrific. It seemed Saxon men really were no better than the Danes.

She wiped her hands over her face, trying to hide her tears. 'They left me for dead,' she said, and anger laced her words now. The anger which had likely been her constant companion these past years, making her the hard, fierce woman she had become. 'And I vowed never to let a man take advantage of me again.'

He wanted to reach for her, to comfort her, but she was so deep into her harrowing tale he wasn't sure she'd want him to. Especially now he knew why she'd shied away from him and his touch. She no doubt saw it as something to be feared.

'It took a long time for me to recover. They'd hurt me. Badly. I decided that when I was strong enough I'd make those men pay for what they did. I spent most of my days learning to fight, so that the next

he couldn't believe she'd ridden out with a convoy of Saxon men to the forest, or insisted on coming with him to Braewood when she must have been downright scared. *Damn*. If he'd known all this he would have been more careful of her feelings.

'And I can honestly say I have never wanted any man's attention. Ever...' A crease appeared in her brow. 'Until now.' She found that mark on the floor again and scuffed her toe against it. 'These feelings I have when I'm with you... They frighten me.'

He studied her beautiful face, now fully understanding her behaviour. She wanted him, as he wanted her, but she was confused. And afraid. And he could see why. If only he'd realised the extent of the trauma she'd suffered before he'd kissed her on the beach... Yet she'd wriggled and writhed against him, encouraging him, enticing him into taking things further, thinking it was what she wanted—and then she'd panicked.

His large arms came around her, pulling her into his chest. He didn't want her to be scared of him. He would have to prove to her that he was trustworthy, that he could be gentle, that he would never hurt her.

'What are you—?'

'Just holding you. Nothing more. You're safe with me, Svea.'

He hoped she knew him well enough by now to realise that this was only to show her he cared—nothing more. He just wanted to give her the comfort she needed.

And to his relief, after a long moment, her body

Our people…we believe such teeth offer protection. I was worried about you when you were gone. I thought you could wear it to keep you safe.'

He smiled, and she could tell she had stirred his emotions. As he reached out to take it from her gratefully, his fingers brushed against hers. Tingles rippled through her again, and she was surprised to still be feeling desire for him, despite what had happened on the beach. Even after running away from him.

'Thank you. I love it.' And, as if to prove it, he instantly pulled it over his head. She smiled back. 'But are you sure you don't want to keep it?' he asked.

'No, it's for you.'

'No one's ever given me a gift before.'

She raised her eyebrows. 'Never?'

He shook his head.

'Not even as a child?'

'No.'

She knew he wasn't close to his father, but she was determined to find out about his late mother, too. How could she not have loved him or treated him with kindness? It made her angry, and she hadn't even known the woman.

'Actually, there is something else I was going to ask you for, but now you've given me this I feel greedy,' he said, fingering the necklace as if it was something to be cherished.

Her breath hitched. 'What is it?'

What could this man want from her? She felt as if she would give him anything. Anything he wanted. If she could.

'I'd be honoured.'

'What do you need?'

'You want me to do it now?' she asked, incredulous. He certainly wasn't wasting any time.

'If you're not too tired,' he said. 'I don't know about you, but I'm not ready to sleep just yet.'

'All right.' She smiled. 'Let's do it.'

And she reeled off a list of the things she would need, including a rose thorn, some wood ash and a few herbs.

Ash reluctantly left the room, telling her he'd be back shortly, and thankfully it didn't take him long to return with the things she needed. She felt a flutter of excitement about creating a design on his chest. It would be incredible to do it for this man whom she was starting to care for. It would help to seal the tentative bond they'd created between them.

She quickly made the mixture and gathered everything together on the table before nervously announcing that she was ready.

'Where do you want me?' he asked.

It was an interesting question… She almost responded with a flirtatious remark, but instantly thought better of being so brazen. She was still shaken by what had happened outside. She could still recall the feel of his tongue in her mouth. Did she want that to happen again?

She realised she did—but would he want to kiss her again, after she'd so callously pushed him away before? And, if he did, how far would they get before she panicked again?

She had never worked in such intimate conditions before—on a bed and in candlelight—and she had certainly never been attracted to the person she was marking... She was all too aware of his warm breath fluttering across her cheek, his dark, steady gaze on her face, and her heart began to pound.

'Do you get this close to all your subjects?' he asked lightly, reaching out to curl one of her braids between his fingers.

'No! And do you mind?' she said, pulling her head away. 'I'm trying to concentrate.'

He grinned, as if he knew the impact he was having on her.

She forced herself to apply herself to the task at hand, drew in a deep breath, and began drawing the outline of her design.

It took a while to get the knotwork just right, and the shading to her liking, but after a while the pattern began to take shape. It started to take on a life of its own. Ash seemed to drift away with his thoughts, allowing her to focus, and she felt as if it was going to be her best work as she poured her heart and soul into it.

She was so glad she'd told Ash about her past. She knew she couldn't be with him without him knowing the truth, and she realised she did want to be with him. No man had ever made her feel this way before. No man had attracted her as he had. And no man had been so strong, yet so gentle. And although he was a Saxon, and she was Dane, and she wasn't sure what future they could have together, she still *wanted*...

His skin was warm and sticky beneath her touch,

blushed. 'Also like you. Each day Odin sends them off around the world to ask questions and garner wisdom and knowledge. That's like you, too. You're always asking questions,' Svea added, talking quickly now, almost babbling. She still couldn't be sure if he liked the design or not. 'They represent power, offer protection, and strike fear into your enemies.'

She swallowed.

He came back to sit next to her on the bed. 'Svea, they're perfect,' he said, looking down at them, unable to take his eyes off the creatures, stroking his fingers over them in awe. 'They say everything I want them to say and more. Thank you. I think you're very talented.'

'Do you really like them?'

'I couldn't have chosen better myself.' He reached out to stroke a long, tanned finger down her face. 'And I think I like myself more with a part of you on me.'

'I liked myself more after I'd covered my skin in patterns. After Crowe. It was as if I was somehow claiming my body back for myself.'

His lips thinned into a hard line at the mention of that man and he took her hand in his. 'Svea, thank you for telling me about what happened. For helping me to understand. I'm truly sorry I stopped you on the battlefield that day, meaning you didn't deal with him as you wanted to.'

'I did, though. Just seeing him, facing him again, made me feel stronger. Watching him fall to his knees, seeing him so weak…and then knowing you'd

every day, thinking it would grow up to be a monster, just like them…'

Ash nodded, but his features tightened and his body tensed, just as it had on the horse the other day, before he'd got down. He looked almost crestfallen. Had she said something wrong again?

He stood, dropping her hand and slowly pushing himself away from her, and she instantly felt the distance. He picked up his tunic and pulled it on, covering up his ink and his beautiful body, and headed towards the door. She realised he was about to leave, and she didn't want him to. She wanted him to stay. But he obviously had other ideas.

Had she said something to put him off? Her mind raced for an explanation. Why was he suddenly trying to get away from her as fast as he possibly could? She shook her head, as if she'd missed something. Something important. Was it because she'd confessed that she was unable to conceive? Did that matter to him? Did that change things? Perhaps he no longer saw her as womanly…

'I'm sorry for all the injustice you've suffered at the hands of men, Svea.' He bowed his head. 'No one should have had to endure what you've been through.' He pulled open the door. 'It's late. I will leave you now to get some rest. It's going to be a long day tomorrow.'

And then he was gone. He walked out into the dark corridor and closed the door behind him and she felt robbed, deprived… She didn't know what she'd been hoping for, but after the intimacy they'd

Chapter Seven

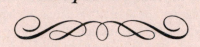

Ash stared at himself in the polished metal slab on his table. Hauling off his tunic and throwing it on the floor, he took in the new design on his skin and ran his fingers over the lines. For a long while, lying on Svea's bed, letting her brand him with her creative gift, he'd thought he had never been so at peace. So content. It had been a beautiful, private time between them, when they'd let their guards down and accepted a mutual trust between them.

He had never wanted her to finish. And yet when he'd seen the exquisite design that captured his whole self so perfectly he had been overwhelmed. As Svea had explained the design he'd heard the words she'd used to describe him... *Thoughtful. Wise. Sensible...* His heart had bloomed. He knew he tried his best. *Passionate. Powerful. Protector...* She knew he would do anything to keep her safe.

He had so desperately wanted to believe that he was all those things she believed him to be. And then... *Monster...*

His lips twisted—at least she was honest. And she was more interested in discovering things about him than anyone had been before, although he knew she shouldn't be. He should have kept his distance... made sure she stayed away. He wasn't good. Not for her. Not for anyone.

Even so, he held the door open wider for her and she ducked under his arm and came inside. He closed the door and leaned against it, feeling at a loss as she stood in the middle of his room, wringing her hands. The place was a mess, his tunic discarded on the floor alongside his boots and sword. What was she doing here? And why had he let her in? He was playing a dangerous game.

'I like your chair,' she said, pointing to the corner. 'And you have a wonderful view of the beach,' she babbled, motioning to the other wall.

'I know,' he said darkly. Surely she wasn't here to talk about his furniture or the pretty scenery outside? 'It's late, Svea. What is it that you want?'

She screwed up her face and he winced at his harsh tone, his direct words.

'Ash,' she said, turning round to face him. 'Did I say—or do—something wrong?'

'No.'

'Is it the ink—do you not like it?'

'It's not the ink, Svea. I told you. It's perfect.'
You're perfect.

'Was it what I said about me being unable to conceive? Does that matter to you? Does it make me somehow less attractive?'

Was that how he'd made her feel? He was such a fool.

He raked a hand through his hair before reaching out to gently grasp her upper arm, wanting to reassure her. 'Svea, you know that I want you. More than anything...' His voice didn't sound real.

'Then kiss me. Please, Ash.'

He squeezed his eyes shut for a second. He wanted to. He really did. But she had been so honest with him—she had laid herself bare, all her scars and insecurities. He was in awe of her bravery. Because he was still lying to her. He was lying about who he really was. And if he'd disliked himself before, he despised himself now. He knew there was no way he could lay a hand on her without her knowing the truth about him. It just wouldn't be fair.

He searched her face for answers, but even as he was trying to muster up the strength to push her away, to let her down gently, he watched her as she fumbled with the fastenings at the neck of her nightgown, untying the collar, her fingers trembling.

His heart was in his mouth. There was nothing he wanted more than to peel away her clothes and explore her beautiful body, to show her how she deserved to be treated, how pleasurable touch could be. And yet if she knew his story—knew what blood he had flowing through his veins, what his father had done—would she still want him?

He covered her hand with his. 'Svea, no.'

She shrank back. Her eyes were filled with confusion, darkened with hurt. He knew he had to tell

Svea frowned, confused.

He knew it was a strange way to start a story, but if he could just make her see… 'Those little cuckoo chicks are monsters. They kill all the others to survive.' He stroked a hand over his beard, hoping the picture he was painting would help with getting his message across.

But Svea shook her head. 'Ash, what are you talking about?'

He swallowed. 'That baby you said you could never have…by one of those men… You said it would have been a monster child.' He took a deep breath. 'Svea, what I'm trying to tell you is *I* was such a child.'

Her breath caught. 'What?'

'Those drawings you saw in my father's chronicles… You're a clever woman—I'm sure you worked it out. Danes attacked our shores years ago, when my father and mother had just married. It was swift and brutal. The people of the settlement didn't stand a chance. One night, when they were asleep in their beds, savage warriors landed on Braewood beach and raced up to the fort, destroying everything in their path, setting the keep on fire. They took some of the women and children with them—presumably as slaves—and killed many of the men. And what Crowe did to you—the way he attacked you—that's what a Dane did to my mother.'

Svea's wide-eyed horrified gaze studied his face as if he'd removed a mask and she was seeing the real him for the first time. She was searching his eyes as he had been doing moments before she'd knocked on the door. Perhaps she was looking for clues to his

through him. But then he came back to the bed, unable to keep his distance from her, his hands on his hips. And now he could add a sense of misgiving and foreboding apprehension to the mix of his feelings, because he was wondering what Svea was thinking. He was desperate to know.

'I was happy living a solitary, reclusive life until recently, when I met you. You wanted to know why I don't live here... It's because I don't feel worthy. I was never made to feel I belonged in Braewood. This place has never felt like my home because I was banished from here when I was a small boy, when my own family couldn't bear the sight of me. Neither could the monks at the monastery I was sent to. They believed I was a devil child. So they made me pay for the crime of being born every single day. Of course my father commanded that my lineage be kept secret in Braewood, for the sake of his pride and the family's reputation, so no one knows the truth—but I do. I feel it. I've felt like an outsider for my whole life. People stare at me as if they know I'm different. And when I see the crumbling keep, the blackened turrets—they're a constant reminder of what happened, of what I am. A monster.'

'No!' Svea shook her head fiercely, her face pale, a tear streaking down her face. 'You're not a monster, Ash. You can't honestly believe that. I know I don't.'

'You said it yourself! You said you wouldn't have wanted a child knowing it was born out of violence. Well, that's what I am... Take a good look. Even my own mother couldn't love me.'

wanted to hear more of the affirming words she was saying. He needed to hear them from her. She was such a positive force in his life. He'd never liked himself very much, but he knew he needed her approval as he needed the very air that he breathed. And if he was to touch her, to make love to her, he needed her consent.

'If you want to know what I see when I look at you, I'll tell you,' she said. 'I see a brave, strong man who is loyal to his King, to his family and his people. A man who cares about others, whether they're Saxon or Dane. A man who is more beautiful, inside and out, than anyone I've ever met before. A man I can trust, wholeheartedly. Please don't push me away, Ash, because of something that happened years ago—before our time. Not when I've never wanted any man to touch me like I do you.'

She bravely pressed her body against him and he rested his forehead against hers.

'Just for one night, Ash, can't we try to forget about who and what we are?'

A hectic beat started clamouring in his chest. He couldn't believe it. He couldn't believe she was saying she still wanted him after all he'd told her. She wasn't repelled or disgusted as he'd thought she might be, which meant she was either insane or he was, to still be standing there, while she was in his room, asking him to lay his hands on her.

And then, in case he needed it spelled out for him, she pulled him down next to her and sat on the edge of the bed again.

ment, hesitation… He wanted her to learn all the soft and hard ridges of his body, and then she wouldn't be afraid of him.

'I like it that there's a part of me etched into your body…' She smiled. 'Forever.'

'Me, too,' he said, kissing her forehead before pulling her beautiful mouth back down to his and letting his tongue become more demanding, more inquisitive, until she was responding, pressing her body closer to his. 'I want to give you something you'll remember forever, too.'

He broke away to leave a trail of delicate kisses down the column of her neck, wanting to probe and examine every part of her with his tongue. He glided it over her swirling patterns, following the lines there, and then down over her collarbone, and the pulse flickering at the base of her throat. Drawing the collar of her gown aside, exposing more skin, he let his hands curve down over the thin material. Carefully, he took one of her breasts in his hand, cupping its weight, and she gasped when his tongue followed in hot pursuit over her swollen skin.

He stared up into her eyes. 'Shall I take this off?' he asked, his hands smoothing over the material that was suddenly annoyingly in the way. He didn't want there to be any barrier between them.

She nodded, her cheeks flushing, and he pulled her up to a sitting position. She wriggled the material free of her bottom and then he took over and lifted her arms up in the air, bringing the gown over her head before discarding it on the floor.

her with his hands, but he knew the delayed gratification would be worth it. It was the most passionate kiss he'd ever experienced, and it soon had her pressing her naked thighs together, squirming against him. He was desperate to touch her there, to push his hand between those delicate blonde curls, nudge between her legs and seek out her intimate places. But he knew he had to show restraint. He had to wait until she was ready.

He moved to her temple, to place soft, sweet kisses there, and then down to nuzzle her ear, his slow torment causing her to thrust her breasts towards him, wanting more. The temptation of her dark, hard nipples was too much. He was drawn to them, wanting them in his mouth, between his teeth, and he groaned. His tongue glided over her naked shoulder, over her collarbone and then down, his open-mouthed kisses laving her perfect breasts, and she writhed beneath him. He sucked a dark, tantalising bud into his mouth, gently dragging his teeth over the slick skin, and she gasped.

Her fingers roamed through his hair, holding him in place, as if she never wanted him to stop. But he had another destination in mind, and as his head lowered, his tongue swirling over the smooth, sensitive skin of her stomach, her hands gripped onto his shoulders.

He moved even lower, and she gasped, trying to sit up, to stop his descent.

'Ash, what are you doing?'

'It will feel nice. I promise.'

The exquisite sensations building inside her were intense, like a restless tide rolling, swelling…and she was riding the crest of his wave. As his masterful tongue glided all the way along her crease with breathless precision, seeking out her core, the wave crashed and shattered into a million pieces against his mouth, the release so extreme she thrashed about in wild abandon, holding his head in place and crying out his name.

It took a while for her body to stop shuddering, and she didn't know how long they lay like that, neither of them moving, his head resting on her thigh. He must be giving her time to get her breath back, but she wanted him to come up, to hold her in his arms again, so she tugged at his shoulder.

He dragged his body up towards her and grinned. 'Was that so bad?'

She blushed, draping an arm across her forehead as he kissed her again. 'You know it wasn't. I didn't realise such a thing was even possible.'

He grinned. 'There's a whole world of possibilities I want to show you, Svea, if you'll let me.' He splayed a possessive hand over her breast.

She giggled. 'Did they teach you to do that in the monastery?'

He grinned. 'Not exactly. I don't think Abbot Æbbe would have approved.'

She sobered. 'Was it all bad…while you were there?' She couldn't bear to think of him being mistreated. She ran her fingers over the scars on his chest. 'Is that where you got these?'

His fingers were so gentle it made her shiver. 'What's that one?' she murmured.

'That's Wynn—meaning hope…joy…perfection. And one more,' he said, drawing a line with two small diagonal lines coming off it. 'This one is Ansuz, known as the Rune of the Ash.'

She smiled up at him. 'I like that one. I like them all.'

'So no, the monastery wasn't all bad. I think the worst thing was feeling so alone. And, of course, not being by the sea. I missed the ocean.'

'I would miss that, too. But Termarth isn't by the sea…' she said thoughtfully. 'Do you like it there?'

'I like the people.' He continued to stroke her back with his fingertips. 'They have come to mean something to me.'

'You know, there were rumours at one time that you were going to marry the Princess.'

He raised his head off the bed. 'Anne?' he asked, surprised.

'Yes. Brand was not happy. I think he felt threatened.'

Ash grinned. Slowly his fingers roamed down to squeeze her soft, smooth bottom, kneading the sensitive flesh.

'He didn't have anything to worry about. There was never anything between us. It seems I prefer my women on the wilder side.' He kissed her lips again. 'And I want to see how wild I can make you, Svea.'

As if wanting better access to her secret places, he pulled her on top of him, so his fingers could dip

had just taken. Not that he'd given her much choice. But she knew now that she must. She wanted to please him, more than anything, but she didn't know what to do. She suddenly wished she'd listened to the women talking about their men and what pleased them back at home, in the longhouse. But she'd always shied away from such conversations.

How ridiculous, she thought, that she was suddenly more nervous, more fearful of this—of wanting to please a man—than of fighting in a battle or running a fortress. Tentatively, she moved to the side of his body, let her hand cover the ridge in his breeches, her fingers trembling. His breath caught.

'Ash,' she said. 'Will you show me what to do... what you like? I want to please you.'

As if all her wishes were coming true, he tugged down his breeches so they were both naked, and she enjoyed the feel of her bare legs entwined with his. He rearranged their position, drawing her back into his chest, her bare bottom pressed against his body. And then he took her hand in his and wrapped her fingers around his shaft.

Kissing her neck, he showed her how to move her hand up and down, and he groaned. She continued to move her hand as he'd demonstrated, and he brushed her hair aside so that he could kiss her neck, her shoulder.

When she ran her thumb over the top of him, experimenting, he gripped her body tighter, his muscles bunching. She thought he must like it, so she did it again.

'Do you want me to stop?'

'No,' she said, and she took a deep breath, willing her tight, tense body to relax around him, to welcome him in. 'Please don't stop, Ash.'

And as he stroked and soothed her, whispering how beautiful she was into her ear, she slowly began to relax around him and he edged further inside. Her breath caught, but this time it was a gasp of pleasure, not pain, and she felt a ripple of heat flood through her. Suddenly she wanted more, gripping his thighs, tugging him towards her, and with a single sudden thrust he slid deep inside her. All the way.

'Svea…?'

'It feels good. *You* feel good.' She had never imagined it could feel like this, and she felt a swell of emotion bloom within her.

He rolled her onto her stomach, so that he lay on top of her, and surged inside her again, making her cry out in wonder at the unexpected, insane pleasure rocking through her. She spread her legs wider and he thrust harder, pinning her to the bed. But she welcomed it now. This was her choice. She wanted Ash to take ownership of her body. She wanted it to be branded with his touch. She wanted to be completely and utterly impaled by her beautiful half-Dane.

He continued to kiss her neck, her shoulder, stroking his hands down her body as she grabbed a fistful of the furs above her head. And then his fingers roamed down, digging into her hips and pulling her up slightly, so he could move his hand beneath her, between her legs. Ruthlessly he pressed his finger

Chapter Eight

When Svea next woke, the sun was streaming through the smoke hole, lighting up the room as Ash had lit up her world last night. She gave a satisfied stretch of her aching muscles. Despite the heaviness of her limbs she felt as if she was floating…lighter than she'd felt in a long, long time. She luxuriated in the memory of their lovemaking, and turned, expecting to find Ash lying in the bed beside her, wanting to ask to do it all again, but he wasn't there. The large bed was empty.

She sat bolt upright and scoured the room with her eyes, but he wasn't there. If it hadn't been for the raw ache between her legs, reminding her of the intimate things they'd done together, she might have thought she'd been dreaming. Instead she smiled. She felt wonderful, elated. But where was he? Had she overslept? When had he left her? And why hadn't he woken her?

She dashed out of bed and snatched up her gown from the floor. She threw it over her, then reached for

'Oh, yes, he said to tell you he knows you'd want to come, but he doesn't want you getting hurt. He said it's best you stay here, where you'll be safe, until he returns.'

Betrayal clawed through her chest like a giant wolf, fighting its way out, and a rage strong enough to set another fire burning through Braewood Keep took hold of her. Thus far they had been a team. She'd thought they had formed a plan to help the King, his men and her friends, and they would see it through together. But he'd left without her, as if he didn't need her. How could he?

She dropped down on to a bench to steady her shaking legs. Yes, she was a woman. But first and foremost she was a warrior and protector of Kald. She wanted to fight for her people. She wanted to be useful—not some feeble Lady who stayed at home, waiting for her man to return. She couldn't believe he was denying her this opportunity, denying her honour. Did he not know what was important to her—did he not know her at all?

And surely he would want her with him at his side? Especially after everything they'd been through? After everything they'd done together last night? If it had been up to her, she wouldn't have been able to let him out of her sight.

She knew what Ellette had told her was true—that Ash probably was worried about her and wanted to protect her and keep her safe—but even so she felt hurt and let down.

Cold, hard determination settled in her stomach.

about which direction Termarth was from here, and how many men had joined Ash today. She readied a horse in the stables and mounted the animal, a fierce conviction solidifying inside her.

Ellette fretted about her, trying her best to persuade her not to go, but she'd made up her mind. She was unshakeable on the matter. And if anything were to happen to her at least she would know she'd tried to make a difference, that she'd been a part of something.

She said goodbye to Ellette and some of the Danish settlers, then spurred the horse on and exited the gates. She instantly found the trail and followed the footprints through the mud, galloping at speed across undulating landscapes, leaving the glittering blue-green ocean behind in the distance. The countryside was vibrant and beautiful, a rainbow of rich colours underneath the crisp sunlight, but she didn't have time to stop and admire the view.

She realised she was finally getting the ride she wanted, and a taste of freedom—only it wasn't along her beloved shoreline at home. She was heading towards enemy territory. But she wasn't afraid. No, what frightened her was the fact that, despite her anger towards him, she was still desperate to see Ash. She wanted to look into his eyes and see if he felt the same as she did after last night. That it had been incredible. Life-altering. She wanted to know that he didn't have any regrets.

She could still feel the taste of his lips on hers, the touch of his burning skin, his long fingers gently

ing her perceptions and her opinions? And as she passed fields of cows, with cute little calves at their hooves, for the first time in her life she wondered what it would be like to be a mother, to have a child to cherish and a husband at her side.

The direction of her thinking scared her. She had spent one night in bed with a man and now she was daydreaming about marriage and children—things that could never be. She was appalled with herself. Hadn't Ash told her himself that he never wanted to marry or have children, and she had repeated the same. She couldn't even conceive. No, their lovemaking had only been for one night. She'd said so herself... Just one night of pure, unequivocal pleasure.

She tried to ground her thoughts, thinking back to the things Ash had told her about his upbringing, and she realised he had never had someone to look after him—not properly. Ellette was probably the closest person he'd ever had to a mother, on those occasions when he'd been allowed to stay in Braewood and see her. Underneath his strict, serious demeanour, she wondered if somewhere there was still a lost little boy, ill at ease with himself? She wondered if her affection could change all that.

She had cared for him when she'd thought he was a Saxon. And she'd wanted him when she'd discovered he was a Dane, too. How could his mother and father not have found something to love in him, as she had? And then she felt cross with herself all over again. What was she thinking? She needed to stir up her anger towards him.

She pulled her shoulders back and held her chin high. She'd done it. She'd made it. She'd show him…

The horse seemed to sense the end of their journey was near and upped his pace for the final few fields that stood between them and their destination. But Svea was suddenly wishing he wouldn't be so speedy. She even found herself reining him back, slowing him down, as she wondered what Ash would say when he saw her.

Suddenly nervous, she had the feeling he wouldn't like the fact she'd gone against his orders. Or that she'd ridden a day across open countryside on her own. No doubt he would call her foolish, and reckless. But why did she care? She was angry with him.

The last thing she wanted him to think was that she had traversed hills and ravines at breakneck speed just to see him, though. Because that would be madness. No, she thought, thinking back to how she'd felt when Ellette had said he'd left without her that morning, stirring the rage that was still simmering in her stomach. She needed to make it clear she was only here to save her men. They were her priority. She was here for the fight.

The camp was a flurry of activity. Ash's men were putting up tents, and the leading Lords were huddled inside the central pitch, discussing the ways in and out of Termarth Castle.

Ash knew the kingdom and all its strengths and weaknesses better than anyone—he had prided himself on learning every entrance, every crack and crev-

he would be able to focus better without her being here, because he wouldn't have to worry about her.

Only he couldn't seem to concentrate at all. His thoughts kept returning to the weight of her breasts in his hands, the taste of her under his tongue and the feel of him moving inside her. He hoped she was all right. He hoped that when this was all over and he returned she would be able to understand his reasons and forgive him. If only he could rescue her men, she might even be proud of him.

A commotion near the gate of the barbican drew his attention and he stood quickly, making his way through the throng of men to see what was going on. The soldiers parted for him as he strode forward and he finally broke through the lines, his hand on the hilt of his sword, ready to face whoever had arrived.

Shock, quickly followed by a rush of joy, jolted through him.

It was Svea.

Svea was dismounting from a large black stallion and the men were leering and laughing, surrounding her, delighted to have a beautiful woman in their midst. They were all trying to help her descend, welcoming her to the camp.

His breath caught. He blinked, as if he didn't believe what he was seeing. But when he opened his eyes again she was still standing there, like a vision of strength and beauty, holding her sword and shield. Pleasure ripped through him. She was here, as if he'd dreamt her into life, so he wouldn't have to wallow in his misery at being apart from her any longer.

When they realised their leader was dealing with the woman they began to disperse, seeming to lose interest. Good. He needed to talk to her, to scold her, and he didn't want an audience.

When they had reached a fair distance away, she flung herself out of his grasp and rounded on him, anger blazing in her blue eyes.

'How could you?' she spat, more enraged than he had thought possible. 'You lied to me, Ash. You made me believe we would do this together.'

'I changed my mind.'

'You can't do that. This isn't about you. It's about your men. My men. Your King. You told me yourself I fight as well as any of your men, and you need every warrior you can get. So why did you leave me behind?'

'You know why,' he barked. 'I don't want you fighting.' He thought he would do anything to ensure her safety. He'd even put her before his King. 'I don't want you out here, among all these men, in the camp or on the battlefield.'

'It's not your choice to make.'

'It's no place for a woman.'

She reeled back at his words. *'No place for a woman?'*

'No. I made a mistake last time in letting you come. I should have stood my ground all those days ago when we rode out from Kald. I've regretted it ever since.'

She gasped.

'You should never have left home that morning. Catastrophe has followed us ever since,' he bit out.

the one who is at fault here. Do you do this with all your women? Make love to them, then leave without even so much as a goodbye?'

'Svea?'

They both turned in the direction of the familiar voice. Shock and surprise crossed Svea's face until pure joy won over them. All her anger dispersed and her face lit up.

'Brand!'

Ash watched as she suddenly turned from him and ran into the Northman's arms. Brand clasped her close. A bolt of jealousy churned in his stomach. It was the scene he'd dreamed of moments before—only she was launching herself into her brother's arms, not his.

'Hi, Sis.'

He hoped beyond hope that the formidable Danish warrior hadn't heard their argument. He didn't think Brand would be too happy to learn that Ash had seduced his sister. And he felt like a brute, because what she'd said was true. He *had* made love to her, then left her without so much as an explanation or a goodbye. Perhaps it was cowardly. But he had done it for her own good.

He felt so damn frustrated—with her and himself. The last thing he wanted was to argue with her, and he hadn't meant what he'd said about regretting that she'd ever left Kald. To regret that would mean he wished last night had never happened, and he wouldn't change that for the world. It had been the best night of his life.

about it, is there? Come on, Sis,' he said, turning to Svea and draping an arm around her shoulder, leading her away. 'Let us get you some ale. And perhaps you can fill me in on what you and Lord Stanton have been up to these past few days.'

Ash and the ealdorman and the other Lords, along with some of Brand's men from Kald, were gathered around the campfire. Brand had shown Svea to the food area and she'd devoured a bowl of stew. Then they'd found her a tent of her own to sleep in by moving some of the men. Now her brother had begun introducing her to the Lords.

Svea was overjoyed to see Brand. She was sorry he'd had to call an early halt to his honeymoon, but she knew they'd have a better chance of rescuing their men, and the King, with him at their side. And when he told her he'd taken Anne back to Kald, and everyone there was safe, she had almost wept with relief. She hadn't realised how worried she'd been. She would have blamed herself if anything had happened there while she'd been away.

She'd filled him in on most of the details—how they'd left Kald and been ambushed, and how Ash had saved her life not once, but twice. She'd even described how they'd decided to head to Braewood to raise the *fyrd*, only leaving out a few minor things— like how she thought she was falling for Ash, the way he made her feel, and the fact that he'd kissed her and made love to her all last night...

She looked across the fire at Ash now, and he was

to him, or touch him, was torture. She wanted to know what he was thinking. She hated to admit it, but she would give anything to be in his arms again. She didn't know what was going to happen out on the battlefield tomorrow, and she had an urge to make every second count. She was starting to feel as if she'd wasted too much time in her life already.

She was glad he'd rallied the troops to fight—he'd done well—and yet she couldn't help wishing they were alone. What she wouldn't give to be back in that grove with him now, just the two of them, or back in his bed, in his strong embrace. She couldn't make sense of her feelings. How could she still want him when she was so angry with him?

She wiped her hands over her face and, suddenly feeling weary, knowing they had a big day ahead of them tomorrow, stood and bade them all goodnight.

'Do you need some help finding your tent in the dark?' Lord Fiske asked, rising alongside her. 'I'd be happy to escort you.'

Ash was up like a shot, his movement sudden, sharp. But Brand spoke words to appease him, to steady his breathing.

'There's no need for that, Lord Fiske,' Brand said, getting out of his seat slowly. 'I'm heading that way myself.'

Looking between Ash and Brand, knowing better than to make a scene, or reveal to the Lords that there was anything between her and Lord Stanton, Svea looped her hand through her brother's arm and

you're angry with him for what he did, for leaving you behind, but I believe he has your best interests at heart.'

'I know that.'

Brand had told her Lord Stanton was a good man back in Kald, when he'd asked her to escort him and their guests to the forest. He'd warned her to be nice. She had known Brand was a good judge of character, but still she'd felt irritated, not wanting to give the Saxon Lord the time of day. She'd wanted to rebel. But now... Now she felt differently. She knew Lord Stanton's deepest, darkest fears, and she knew how he felt when he moved inside her.

'I know you want to fight, Svea. And I'm not going to deny you that chance. We need your skills. But I also know how much I care about Anne, and I wouldn't want her anywhere near this place... I can understand how Lord Stanton feels.'

'What are you saying?'

Had he seen something between them?

'Just that maybe he had good reason to act the way he did. When you care about someone, you'll do anything to protect them. Don't stay cross with him forever. Life's too short.'

She nodded, swallowing the lump in her throat. She knew he was right.

'Goodnight, Svea.'

She watched him go, before giving a heavy sigh and passing through the cloth door of her tent. A hand on her arm startled her, spinning her round, and she gasped.

me when I say it comes from my fear of you getting hurt. Of my not being able to protect you.'

His fingers stole down between her legs and she knew he must have found her damp. She knew that she was. She writhed against his hand.

'I never asked for your protection, Ash.'

He stroked her fiercely through the material and her legs buckled, so he pushed a muscled thigh between hers.

'I know that, but you have it anyway. Watching you sleeping naked in my bed, you looked so perfect, too precious to take into battle. I need to know you'll be safe.'

'You have to take risks in life, Ash. Like I did with you last night.'

'Were you sore this morning?' he asked, softening his touch.

'No... I just...wanted more. And I turned to find you gone...'

He groaned. 'Please, Svea... Give me permission to pleasure your body. Put me out of my misery. Tell me that you want me inside you again.'

She liked to hear him beg. It gave her confidence a lift.

She tossed her hair back over her shoulders and his arms came up and around her again, pulling her close, trying to trace the soft swells of her breasts. But the cold chainmail of her armour was in his way. She pushed him down onto the bed and stood before him. She unclasped the metal and it fell away. He moved his hands towards her belt, unfastening it, using the

nipples between her fingers, she watched the pulse throb in his neck.

'Svea...'

She thought back to how she'd wanted to ruffle his feathers on the marshland, when she'd barely known him. Well, she was certainly doing that now.

'I have a right to be here, Ash. I'm not like one of your Saxon women. I follow my own desires. You can't tame me.'

She parted her thighs and her hands stole down between her legs. His eyes dilated, his hard cock straining against his breeches as he followed her every movement, clearly not wanting to miss a second of what she was doing.

'Do you know...I touched myself here when I bathed in Braewood? I thought of you.'

'Svea...' he choked.

'I'm thinking of you touching me here now. Do you want to touch me here, Ash?'

She didn't need to ask him twice. As if he could bear it no longer, he launched himself towards her, sinking to his knees, and laid claim to her with his mouth.

His hands came round her to hold her buttocks, to fasten her to him, and she was glad. She didn't think she could stand without his support. His tongue glided along her opening, nipping at her little bud of pleasure, and she held on to his shoulders for dear life. She had him exactly where she wanted him.

The pleasure was mounting, already too much, but she wasn't ready for it to be over—not before he

He groaned loudly. His hands twisted into her hair, bringing her mouth down further onto him. She had no idea what she was doing—she just knew she wanted to torture him as he was her. She wanted to send him to the brink. She wanted to set him free, make him wild. She took him to the back of her throat and he swore. She smiled and did it again, and he bucked beneath her. Oh, yes, he'd definitely lost that cool control now. All restraint was gone.

All at once, in a swift movement, he growled and pushed her down onto her back, lowering her so she was stretched out beneath him on the floor. And he parted her thighs wide with his legs.

'Is this all right?' he asked, as his large body hovered over her.

She appreciated that he was checking on her, but she wasn't afraid any more. She just needed him. 'Yes. I want you. Now, Ash.'

She lifted her arms to place her hands around his neck, pulling him down on top of her, and then he was right there, at her entrance. He used his hard, silky tip to stroke up and down her crease, opening her up to him, and as his tongue probed inside her mouth he guided his cock inside her. Every muscle in her body tensed at the invasion, the blinding pleasure, and she bit down on his lip to stop herself from screaming out. He felt huge inside her body, filling her up, and incredible. He thrust again, beginning to up the pace, moving faster, longer, harder, deeper. But she still wanted more. She wanted everything he could give.

Her arms roamed down his back to grip his bot-

Chapter Nine

More than a hundred warriors raised their huge wooden shields as they lined up to create a wall on the plains outside Termarth. It would be a formidable sight to their enemy, and yet Ash couldn't help wishing they were on the other side of the imposing stone ramparts.

He knew this place inside out, and defending it from the outside was a bizarre prospect. One he had never imagined possible. He felt as if he had let down all the people within the walls.

Sworn to protect them, he had left the kingdom undefended when he'd travelled with King Eallesborough to Kald for his daughter's wedding. From Ash's own upbringing he knew that you couldn't look after something from afar—it would slip beyond your grip. The distance between him and his parents had become irreparable. And now, just looking at the damage his absence had caused to Braewood and Termarth, it only helped to prove his point.

Saxon rebels had taken the kingdom, and the King

against an ominous ashen sky, and Svea turned to face him. They exchanged a look. He hoped seeing those beasts of battle now etched into his skin was a good omen. He felt the heavy throb of his heartbeat, his muscles tightening in readiness. He hoped he could lead them all to victory.

'Just promise me you'll be careful,' he said, trying not to focus on all the things that could go wrong, already doubting his decision to allow her to make her own choices and fight.

She rolled her eyes. 'I will, Ash. Promise me you will stay safe, too.'

He nodded.

He had slipped from her arms and her bed before dawn this morning. Before anyone had been awake to notice. But it had taken all his strength to leave her. Sprawled out naked between the furs, she had been everything he'd ever dreamt of, all he wanted, and his chest had hurt. He had never had trouble leaving a woman's bed before. He had never wanted to repeat any night he'd spent with one. He had never been interested in sharing confidences or creating intimacy. But this woman…

He couldn't bear her being out of his sight, out of his arms. They belonged together.

Even now, as he urged his horse forward to the gate to request a word with Lord Crowe, he didn't like the distance he was putting between them. If he was apart from her he couldn't protect her. But he tried to focus on the large looming entrance, and on what he was going to say. His words might make all the dif-

But Brand was at her side in an instant, folding her in his arms, smothering her cries, holding her tight.

Ash felt the slow trickle of failure pass through him. This was all his fault. He'd let her down. And he would now have to accept the consequences...the repercussions of his actions.

He stared at the harrowing sight before him. There was one thing Ash now knew with absolute clarity. He knew that Svea had been right—it didn't matter if you were Saxon or Dane, all men could be evil, no matter what blood flowed through their veins. He felt his nostrils flare, his fists clench and unclench. He had to push the pain down, deal with it later and let the rage take over.

It was as if an unspoken understanding had passed between the ealdormen and the warriors. There would be no talking. No negotiation. This was the rallying cry that made these accidental allies come together against one enemy, and they would fight for their lost men, for their King, for vengeance, to the death.

As a loud rumble of thunder ripped across the sky, Svea opened the battle by throwing a spear towards the Saxon on the gate, honouring her god Odin, and then there was no hesitation. All stealth and strategy was cast aside, and with a combined guttural roar they launched into attack, the shield wall of men advancing on the towering fortifications.

Soldiers began to scale the castle walls while storms of sling stones started flying over the ramparts, raining down on them, trying to halt their ascent. Ash and Brand led the cavalry charge to the

smoke choking the fighters, and arrows and bodies ricocheted off the walls as the fight raged on. He just hoped they could salvage the soul of the kingdom after this.

Suddenly a flaming arrow struck a cart behind him, engulfing the men there in flames. Ash's armour burned and he unclipped it, shucking off the hot, heavy metal and his scorched tunic. His skin prickled with pain. He welcomed it. He saw it as punishment.

Seeing their chance to attack him while he was down, a group of Crowe's men approached, surrounding him, but their skills were no match for his fury. He sensed the conflict was turning. They were overpowering their enemy…the fighting was coming to its climax. The men on both sides were tiring, but still they fought on, with a grim determination.

Suddenly realising that Svea was gone, that she wasn't at his side, Ash swung his gaze around the courtyard, over the devastated market stalls and burning food stores, the roofs on fire, wildly searching for her face among the mayhem, his heart pounding in his chest. How had he lost her?

His eyes finally fell upon her on the bridge, but his blood chilled. She was challenging the Crowes, a ferocious look on her face, and he watched the sickening showdown begin to unfold. He couldn't be sure how coming face to face with her attacker would be making her feel—he just knew he needed to get to her. *Now.* He was in awe of her bravery, but aghast at her notion that she could take on two of Calhourn's fierc-

when she was just a young girl. Ash wanted him dead just as much as she did.

'Lord Stanton, I thought we were allies...' Crowe sneered as he continued to tackle Svea. 'Surely you're not going to take the side of a heathen over a friend? Drop your weapon and I'll consider not killing the girl...just hurting her a little. We could even share...'

'Never.'

His hair around his shoulders, his tunic gone, revealing the dark warrior patterns on his chest, Ash realised he looked more like a Northman than ever. And finally, in that moment, he was ready to embrace it.

'You're a traitor to your kind, Stanton,' said Crowe.

'On the contrary. I'm a Northman, and you make me proud to call myself a Dane.'

He glanced down to the courtyard and saw Brand had put down his opponents and was lighting a spindle of arrows. He hoped the King would forgive them for this.

He gave Brand the signal and then yelled, 'Svea—move!'

Instantly, she jabbed her elbow into Crowe's ribs and leapt away. Ash grabbed her and pulled her into his arms, to safety, just as the torrent of firelit arrows hit the bridge, covering the entire entrance to Termarth in flames.

And as the city wall collapsed, taking the Crowes' bodies down with it in an almighty avalanche of wood and stone, the deafening rumbling sound reverberated around the castle, drawing the battle to a close.

distance between them before halting and turning back. 'Just…try not to get into any more trouble while I'm gone.'

Svea nodded, watching him go. Was he all right? She hoped so.

She looked around her in despair, taking in the devastation and destruction. She didn't know what to do first—where to start. Everything was in disarray. Little fires were still burning…bodies were strewn about everywhere. She sank down to her knees amid the chaos. People were wailing, clambering over wood and stones to get to safety, and the farmsteads and grain stores had been burned to the ground.

She had never seen such a bleak sight, and she felt overwhelmingly tired. But she didn't care. *They'd won.* They'd taken down Crowe and his brother and reclaimed the castle. They'd achieved what they'd set out to do all those days before, despite the heartbreaking losses they'd suffered along the way.

Ash had been nothing less than heroic, leading the men into the fray with grit and determination. And he'd rallied the people, encouraging them to take up arms against the enemy. He was right. She'd rushed in again, having seen the Crowes and not wanting to let them out of her sight, not wanting to allow them to get away. But once again she'd been foolish. She should have waited for help, because of course they'd overpowered her. Two against one.

And all those feelings had come rushing to the surface. Fear, yes—but mainly anger. Anger that they

'The King's alive,' he said, coming down beside her, with drizzling rain and a look of sheer relief washing over his features. 'We scoured the castle and found him locked in the dungeons. He's shaken, but unharmed. And he's very grateful to us all for saving his life and his crown.'

Elation ripped through Svea. She was glad the King was safe. It meant all the loss of life hadn't been for nothing. And it would mean a great deal to Ash. She knew how guilty he felt for not saving the King on the marsh, but now he had redeemed himself. Her heart swelled. All would be well.

She stretched out her arms and allowed Brand to lift her to her feet. They began to pick their way through the rubble, trying to find survivors, attempting to clear up some of the mess. The storm dragged on, and despite the cold and wet seeping through their clothes they were glad of the rain, as it helped to put out the fires, halting the damage to the castle walls.

It was a long, painstaking afternoon, which took its toll on their bodies and their thoughts. By nightfall, the King had organised a celebratory feast in the grand hall but despite their victory the mood was sombre. The ordeal of recent weeks had worn them down. The people were weary—they had lost too much.

Looking around the grand hall, adorned with paintings and gold and garnet decorations, rich, soft furnishings and roaring fires, Svea sat in wonder. But none of the trinkets and trophies drew her eye as much as the man at the end of the table, who sat at the side of the King.

ding in Kald. He seemed almost impregnable, sitting there brooding, and it sent a shiver of unease through her body.

She knew he must have a million tasks to do and, knowing him, he would be engaging in them so he didn't have to deal with feelings of grief for his men. She knew now that he was an expert at crushing his emotions, and probably had been since he was that young boy who'd been unloved and abandoned by his parents. But surely he had time to speak to her? To check on her? Surely he wanted to?

Because she wanted to speak to him—she wanted to talk about the day, the battle, to go over the details with him. She wanted to tell him how she'd felt when she'd come face to face with Crowe. She wanted to share her feelings about it with him and hear his in return. But he hadn't even once looked her way. It was as if he was withdrawing from her, from everyone— as if he wanted to be alone. But why?

She found it infuriating. She was hurt, too. She had lost two of her beloved shield brothers, and she needed him. She wanted to seek comfort in his arms and in his bed. Could he not see that? Did he not care?

His eyes were devoid of any emotion, and wary apprehension ebbed through her. This man, sitting so far along the table from her, silent and resolute, wasn't the man who had taken her swimming in the sea and shared laughter with her in the kitchen in Braewood. Nor was he the man who had made passionate love to her last night. No, this man had the weight of the world on his shoulders. Did he not realise he'd suc-

But what if it wasn't that at all? What if it was simply that now they'd seen their mission through he didn't need or want her any more? That, whatever they'd experienced together, he now wanted it to be over? She shuddered at the thought.

Last night, even the delicious meats, the sweet honey-based mead and the music hadn't been able to lift her spirits, and she had been glad when they'd all retreated to their rooms for the night. They were the most luxurious, magnificent spaces she'd ever seen, and yet she knew she would trade it all to be back in Ash's room in Braewood in a heartbeat. She would do anything to be in his arms. And all night, on hearing every footstep or noise outside her door, her heart had jumped, hoping it was him, that he'd finally come to her.

But he hadn't.

She wondered why he'd shut himself down, not speaking to her, keeping her at bay. She had barely slept, and she felt bone-achingly tired. And now, as she and Brand followed the King as he began to climb the stone staircase that led to the battlements, over-looking views of the golden rolling fields, the glowing copper leaves on the trees marking the passing of time, she could no longer bear it. She had to say something.

'King Eallesborough, I hope you don't mind me asking, but have you seen Lord Stanton today?'

Brand glowered at her, as if what she was asking the King wasn't appropriate, but she ignored him, instead focusing on the Saxon monarch. He had a

The King looked up at Brand and Svea before continuing. 'He went on to tell me how his father was a Dane. I'm not sure how I didn't see it before... I mean, now that I know I can see it as clear as day. You can just tell, can't you? Look at the two of you,' he said, and smiled, gesturing to their strong bodies and dark markings.

Svea thought back to the day before, when she'd seen Ash charge towards her on the ramparts. His chest bare, his ink on display for all to see, his extraordinary muscles rippling, he had looked almost superhuman—like a demi-god. But he was a Saxon and a Dane. Her demi-Dane.

'He should have known it wouldn't be a problem to me. My own daughter married a Dane, after all,' he said, standing, placing a hand on Brand's shoulder. 'A good man. But it is to him. He said people knowing will compromise his position here. He thinks it will confuse the soldiers and the people—that they won't know which side he is on. He seemed almost... ashamed.'

Svea winced in pain, as if the King's words were puncturing her body. She knew Ash was worried about the blood he had flowing through his veins, and she had tried to convince him he was no monster. She had thought he was concerned about the actions of his father, the fact that he'd been conceived in rape, and what kind of person that made him. She hadn't thought he was actually *ashamed* of being a Dane. And if that was the case, he was ashamed of the part of him that was like her.

understand. How could he? Would he now agree to his father's demands? Was he contemplating marrying Lady Edith after all? Someone who could give him a child? She felt sick. Would he even say goodbye to her?

Bitterness burned through her body. She knew the differences between them were insurmountable, and she knew she had been insane to think they could ever be together—his father certainly wouldn't allow it, not while he was still alive. And yet there had been a part of her that had foolishly hoped and dreamed… But now those dreams were unravelling. Spiralling away. He was leaving her. Again. But this time she couldn't go after him. Because this was different. She wasn't sure it was her place. She would have to let him go, and she wasn't sure she could endure it.

Excruciating grief rumbled through her and she nearly sank to her knees. It was only her pride that kept her standing.

They'd survived the battle of his lifetime, and they'd been victorious, and yet Ash didn't think he'd ever despised himself more than in this moment as he made his way through the devastated castle square towards Svea.

People congratulated him as he passed them by, applauding his bravery, his win, and he nodded his head in thanks. But inside he'd never felt so defeated.

He had confessed his guilt to the King, over not being able to save him on the marshland in Kald, but King Eallesborough wouldn't hear it, instead spoiling

exhausted from trying to hide it. So now the truth was out.

Sitting in the throne room where the King's witans often took place, his monarch had listened to his story—the one he'd revealed to Svea that night in Braewood—and Ash had been ready to take whatever punishment came his way. But, stroking his hand over his well-groomed beard, the King had just listened, nodding, accepting. He'd merely asked what side Ash would choose if he had to decide between Saxons and Danes, and Ash had replied, 'The right side. The peaceful side.'

Ash had told his King he was stepping down from his position. If *he* wasn't proud of who he was, how could others look up to him? How could he ask others to follow him? How could anyone place their trust in him again? He knew he'd never forgive himself for any of it. Through his actions he'd lost everything. His self-respect. His men. And the woman he loved.

And he would soon lose his father. So he'd come to a decision. He had to go home—back to the place where his life had begun. Now his secret was out his father didn't have that hold over him, and he would try to resolve the differences between them before it was too late. Doing that would at least create the foundation for building a future he was proud of.

Digging into his last reserves, he crossed the final steps to where Svea was standing. It would take the last of his strength to tell her he was leaving, to say goodbye to her. It might just destroy him. But he knew that this time he had to do things right.

she'd said to him the other night, to build him up. He desperately wanted her to tell him not to go…not to leave her. He knew she had the power to sway him.

But of course she didn't.

He hadn't saved her men, as he'd promised. And out there on the ramparts it had been too close. She had almost got herself killed. He'd almost lost her, not been able to protect her. And the fact she'd tried to fight the Crowes by herself, not trusting him to do it, just proved what she really thought.

The silence stretched between them, and he scuffed the floor with his boot. 'How long do you intend to stay in Termarth?' he asked, and he cringed at his own pleasantries, feeling the words drying up on his tongue.

'A few days at most. Brand wants to get back to Anne in Kald as soon as possible.'

At the mention of his name Brand came over to greet them, breaking through some of the tension. 'You're returning to Braewood, Lord Stanton?'

'I am.'

Ash and Brand gripped and shook each other's forearms.

'I wish you a safe and speedy journey. It was an honour to fight with you,' Brand said. 'And I have been meaning to thank you for taking care of my sister while I was gone. For protecting her.'

Ash swallowed. *Not very well.* It was an effort to look into his fellow Northman's eyes. They had fought alongside each other as allies. But Brand knew who he was, what he stood for, whereas Ash had

ing herself into lifting more stones, and Ash had never suffered pain like it. Not on the battlefield, nor at the hands of his father and mother. She wasn't going to say goodbye.

With a final nod to the Northman, he turned on his heel. It took every drop of his willpower to walk away from her, to walk out of her life.

Brand sighed. 'Svea, winter is on its way, and this place is cold enough without you giving us all a chill as well. You're being unusually vile to everyone. We're all used to your feistiness, and we know you can be surly—we've always accepted why—but come on… It's been going on long enough, don't you think? Crowe is dead. You should be moving on with your life. But you seem to be more morose than ever.'

She tried to ignore him, wiping her hands on her pinafore and wrapping her shawl a little tighter around her. She gave an involuntary shudder. Brand was right—it was getting colder. It was going to be a brutal winter.

'A messenger came to the gates today,' he carried on.

'Oh?'

She wished he'd stop talking. She just wanted to get on with readying the dinner. She really didn't feel like making mundane chit-chat.

'The messenger was from Braewood.'

Her hand stilled on the axe for a second as a sharp twinge tore through her chest. Then she reached for another slippery silver fish and started hacking again. Only she felt a slight tremble in her hand. She didn't want to think about Braewood. She didn't want to think about Ash. It hurt too much. And she was angry with herself that just the mention of his name evoked this reaction in her. It had been a few months—she should have forgotten him by now.

'Don't you want to know what the message said?' Brand offered her a questioning gaze.

The axe slipped out of her hand and clattered to the table. 'No.'

Brand couldn't be serious. There was no chance of her going back there—not after the way Ash had left her, without so much as an explanation. Not after she'd discovered he was ashamed of himself as well as of her. And it would be far too humiliating to see him and his no doubt beautiful Saxon bride-to-be together...

'Svea, we're going,' Brand said, rising from his seat and coming towards her.

'You can go. I'm not.'

'He won't think much of that.'

'I don't care what he thinks,' she said, exasperated.

He hadn't cared what she thought when he'd walked out of her life after taking her to bed...after making her long for things she'd never wanted before. She'd hoped he would heal her, but she'd ended up more broken than before. Well, that wasn't strictly true...but it helped to tell herself that to stir up her anger against him, so she wouldn't wish for things she shouldn't.

'Besides, he won't want me there. I'm sure I'm a long-distant memory.'

'You don't believe that and neither do I. I think you owe him this, Svea—it's the least you can do.'

'Me?' Indignant rage shot through her.

'Yes, you! For pity's sake, Svea, he was like a broken man when he walked away from you in Termarth, after you treated him so callously that morning he came to say goodbye.'

ing her stomach and she felt nauseous. She couldn't concentrate.

'As I understand it, his father threatened to disinherit him if he hadn't married and produced an heir by the time he passed away. Lord Stanton hasn't complied with his father's demands—you *do* know that he has refused to marry, don't you?'

She bit her lip, shaking her head. She hadn't wanted to hear anything about Ashford Stanton since the moment he'd walked out of her life and she and Brand had returned to Kald. She'd feared the worst, thinking he must have gone back to Braewood and followed his father's orders. She perhaps should have known better. She knew how stubborn Ash could be...almost as stubborn as her... He had told her he didn't want to marry, and she should have believed him. He had never given her reason to think he would lie.

Brand nodded. 'He refused, and so his father renounced his claim to his lands and titles.'

She swayed on her feet, suddenly feeling lightheaded, so she pulled out a seat and sat down.

'Are you all right?'

She had been feeling so tired lately. She'd even found her usual enjoyment of her favourite pastimes waning. She'd been struggling to muster up the energy to go riding or swimming, and she was finding cooking for the masses exhausting. It was as if the passing of time had slowed these past few weeks, and everything seemed lacklustre.

'I'm fine. Really.'

'So, because he's been disinherited by his father,

stubbornness stopped her from reaching out to him, preventing him from leaving?

She suddenly felt bereft. And so utterly foolish. But she had no experience in these things. She had never had feelings like this before.

'Oh, Brand. I didn't give him a chance, did I?' She gasped, bringing her hand up to cover her lips. 'I think...I think I was too blinded by my own hurt to see his pain.'

Her brother nodded, and then pulled her into a comforting hug. It was good to be held again. She took a deep breath and let some of her anger go.

'It's never too late, Svea. I still assert that Lord Stanton is a good man, and I believe that my sister, the one I know of old, deserves to be happy. She deserves to be with someone like that. My sister the shield maiden has always fought for what she wants, what she believes in. She's never let anything stand in her way. Even a man's mind.'

Svea felt a coil of cautious hope unfurl in her stomach at hearing Brand's words. Perhaps it was time to take one more risk... Ash had told her he didn't want to marry, and she might not be able to change his mind on that, but she could let him know she didn't hold a grudge against him and make him see that he was a good man. She could be brave and tell him that she would be at his side, no matter what. Unlike his parents, she would be there unconditionally.

Brand stepped away from her, holding her hands in his. 'So...are we going?'

worrying that the truth would come out, it had felt liberating to tell the world who he was. He'd felt like a free man—as if his chains had finally been cast off. He had expected to be shunned by some, and that would be nothing new. And yet here in Braewood the people had rallied round him, supported him. And all that had helped him to accept himself and start to like who he was.

He was glad he'd been with his father at the end. They'd never been close, but he was pleased he had come home for his final few months, during which he had tried to appease the man as best he could. He needed to be sure he'd done all he could to make amends, and he'd conceded to many of the man's wishes—all apart from one.

The burial had been a sombre affair—just the priest, Ash and a few household members. But afterwards they had invited guests into the mead hall for food, singing and dancing, to celebrate the life of the late ruler of Braewood.

Ash thought it strange that this might be the last night he'd spend in the fortress. He realised his emotions had come full circle within these walls. Born out of barbarity, he had suffered a cruel childhood here, and when he'd returned years later, moulded into the man they'd requested he become, he still hadn't been welcome.

But when the walls of Braewood had finally come into view after returning from the battle in Termarth Ash had realised he wasn't feeling his usual aversion to the place. He'd always felt the huge palisades and

and Ash's father's work on building up the walls to make them even higher seemed to have been paused. And there were no Danes camped outside.

She was surprised by how much seeing the place warmed her and lifted her spirits, despite the biting cold. She supposed it was because she had spent the best night of her life here, so it would always have a special place in her heart.

The journey from Kald had been hard going, as a light flurry of snow had begun to cover the ground. And it hadn't been helped by the butterflies in her stomach. Brand had decided they should take the long way, around the forest, and she hadn't argued—she'd actually been relieved.

She didn't want to see familiar landmarks and have her memories stirred. She didn't want to be reminded of all the moments she and Ash had shared together on their journey through the woodland to the coast. Although, looking around, she saw the landscape had changed since they'd escaped across the countryside all those months before, with the trees and hedgerows now barren. All the colours of the scenery seemed to have been leached, washed away, just like her happiness.

As they dismounted their horses and made their way into the fortress her skin was like gooseflesh. But, as much as she couldn't wait to get inside and warm herself by the fire, she was also aware she was hanging back behind Brand and Anne. They had received a warm welcome at the gate, but Svea wondered if Ash would be as receptive, and she was suddenly more nervous than she'd ever been. She

of heat. She was astounded to see the hall was full, buzzing with a mixture of Saxon and Danish people, all mingling. It was a world apart from when she and Ash had sat at the table together alone, sharing an intimate candlelit dinner for two. She thought back to their laughter over the blackberries and smiled to herself.

Svea was delighted to see some of the Danish settlers again, who instantly came to talk to her and were excited to reveal that Ash had built them new farmsteads. They said they were working the land and had their own animals, and were all happier than they'd ever been. Svea was so pleased for them.

Then she saw Ellette, and the woman wrapped her in a fulsome embrace as if she was elated to see her. Svea felt her emotions rising to the surface and tried to swallow them down.

'You look tired, love,' the kind woman said, and ridiculously Svea felt her eyes sting with tears. She thought how amazing it was that you could feel so much warmth towards a person after only having met them once, but it had been during a time of heightened awareness—a time that mattered deeply, and the woman had taken care of her.

They exchanged a few words, and Ellette said that things had improved a great deal since Ash had moved home. Svea was glad. She wanted to ask how he was, and she wanted to ask about Lady Edith, but she couldn't bring herself to utter the words.

'Keep your fingers crossed for Lord Stanton today,' Ellette told her, before rushing off to tend to the cook-

breath. He was here. Taking in his rugged good looks, his molten, dark gaze and his long, loose hair, she thought he looked more handsome than ever before. Love blossomed in her chest and she wanted to stand up and throw her arms around him, tell him how she felt, that she'd never meant to let him go.

But instead she just sat there. She couldn't move. She knew she should say something about being sorry for his loss—anything—but she just couldn't get the words out. For the first time in her life she was rendered mute.

'We were very sorry to hear about your father, Lord Stanton,' said Brand, coming to her rescue.

Svea panicked. How could she even begin to broach the subject of her feelings towards him and close the chasm that had opened up between them when she couldn't even say hello?

Ash nodded, thanking them all for coming, and then, after focusing his gaze on her for another moment, he was gone. He was moving around the room, tending to his other guests, talking animatedly to the men, listening to the women. Her heart felt as if it would shatter. Was that it? Was that all he could say to her? Well, at least he'd said hello, which was more than she'd been able to manage…

Did he not care that she was here? She watched him move about, more at ease with himself than she'd ever seen him—as if he'd grown into himself these past few months…as if he was more comfortable with his body and who he was—and her heart ached. She wanted him to come back. She wanted him to look

Ash.

She had been gone just moments. How did he know she'd sneaked in here? Had he been watching her? Following her? The thought pleased her.

'I hope you're not even contemplating doing any work. You're a guest here.'

She shrugged, the feel of his touch burning her skin. 'I—I wanted to help. I couldn't just sit there, watching you talking to—'

His gaze narrowed on her. 'Come with me.'

He led her out through the back, as he had the night they'd eaten honey on bread and played with the flour. She wanted to return to that moment. It had felt so wonderfully carefree. Although she was suddenly struck with guilt that they'd never cleaned up the mess. Poor Ellette. She would have to make amends…

'Where are we going?'

Ash's hand was gripping her arm too tightly, but she didn't mind. He was here. They were alone. And she never wanted him to let go. Besides, she didn't think she could walk without him holding her up, her legs were trembling so much.

'The beach.'

'Won't you be missed?' she asked.

'I'm sure they can cope without me for a while.'

'Don't think for one minute I'm going for a swim—'

He stopped suddenly, pulling her round to face him so they were just a breath apart. And she was thrilled to be with him again, to have his hands on her skin, but incredibly nervous, too. Her stomach was in knots.

'What can I say? I'm trying to make up for my earlier failures,' he said, his lips curling upwards, although the smile didn't quite reach his eyes. 'You know me... I like to be busy.'

You know me. Her heart clenched. It pained her to hear him say it. It hinted at the past intimacy they'd shared. She'd thought she knew him. She wanted to know everything about him again. Always.

His grip on her arm dropped down to her wrist and he tentatively took her hand in his. How was his skin so warm when it was icy out here?

'Svea, I want to talk about what happened in Termarth. I owe you an apology... I'm sorry that I couldn't save your men. When I saw that cart being wheeled out through the gate, and Kar and Sten among the bodies, it was as if a huge wooden door closed on my life. I felt as if I had let you down. I felt as if I'd let them down.'

She shook her head. 'Their deaths... It was not your fault, Ash. No one could have saved them. Not you, nor I. I know you think their blood is on your hands, but it's not. Please don't hold yourself to impossible standards no one else would place on you.'

His dark gaze considered her. 'But when I left you were angry with me. You seemed to despise me. You didn't say goodbye.'

She never wanted to say goodbye to him. She thought it would break her. 'Yes, I *was* angry with you. But not about that.'

'What, then?' He looked confused.

She glanced down at the sand. She was reminded

couldn't be angry with him for that. For hadn't she done the same? She had sworn to hate all Saxon men, including him. Especially him. And now she realised she had wanted to hate him because she had loved him from the start and her feelings had scared her.

His hand smoothed over the skin on her hand and he brought his other hand up to cup her cheek. 'It took falling in love with a Dane for me to realise the truth. That my parents had got it wrong and you'd got it right. That every person has the potential to be good or bad, no matter if they're Saxon or Dane. And I had started to have hope…to believe I was good. You made me think I really could be. Until I let everyone down…'

'You didn't, Ash.'

'I realised that day out on the ramparts in Termarth that I'd had enough of apologising for who I am. I was ashamed that I'd lied to everyone. I knew then that I had to embrace my heritage—especially if it meant I had a chance to be with you. And I thought the best place to do that was here. I had to lose everything, sacrifice everything, go back to the beginning and find myself. I needed to learn to like myself before I could ask anyone else to love me. Before I came for you. I realised the act of how I came to be no longer mattered, but how I choose to act did.'

He took a step closer towards her, their bodies touching now.

'My father insisted that I must marry a Saxon if I wanted to keep my title and inheritance…'

Svea swallowed. 'Lady Edith is very beautiful.'

But he had changed her—she saw that now. Whereas once she had been fierce and reckless, he had calmed her, taught her how to be gentle. He'd broken her in and she had adapted to his touch. And she wanted to be his, as he was saying he was hers. Forever.

'Then, yes, I'll marry you, Ash. Of course I will. I love you.'

A shout from the cliff above broke through their total absorption with one another. 'Lord Stanton, your presence has been requested in the hall. The witan have voted and made their decision. Please, come quickly.'

Nerves bunched in Svea's stomach. She hoped the ealdormen had made the right choice. That they had put their faith in Ash to lead them forward into a brighter future, as had she. But she knew, whatever the outcome, they would get through it together.

Svea began to move, to step away, to make her way up the path towards the fortress, but Ash gripped her, tugging her back towards him.

'Don't you want to go and find out—?'

'It can wait,' he said, pulling her up against him hard, bringing his lips down onto hers.

It started as a soft, slow kiss as he reacquainted himself with the feel of her mouth, his tongue caressing hers in a sensual bone-melting way, and then it deepened to become proprietorial, passionate, so unrestrained it left her breathless and achingly incomplete.

'Now we can go.'

He grinned, lifting his head away and pulling her

ish bride. And she thought her heart might just burst with joy.

Everything was perfect. *Almost.* There was just one thing niggling her... But as people came to congratulate them and wish them well she tried to bury it, telling herself she'd deal with it later. She couldn't ruin this moment.

Brand was ecstatic for them, of course, spinning her around and telling her how happy he was for her, and he and Ash had taken themselves off to discuss the arrangements, their arms around each other's shoulders like brothers.

The drinking and merriment went on long into the evening, until finally people retired to their rooms or farmsteads, and others passed out on benches or curled up by the fire.

Staring down into her eyes, Ash took Svea's hand in his before leading her down the corridor to his room. The flutters of excitement low in her stomach, between her legs, were getting more fierce the closer they got to being alone. And the instant the door closed behind them they were in each other's arms, their mouths sealed together, tearing at each other's clothes.

Ash practically ripped her dress from her shoulder on one side, so desperate was his need to have her naked in his arms again, and she fell against him, laughing. One breast sprang free from the confines of the material and, holding her hands in his, behind her arching back, he let his mouth work its way down her neck to her heaving chest as he hardened against her

world if it was going to be anything like me. Why? Why are you asking now?'

'Do you remember whát I told you?' she said, chewing her bottom lip. 'About what the healer said to me?'

He nodded, his brow furrowing deeper. 'She said she wasn't sure you'd ever be able to have children after what happened to you in Termarth...'

She swallowed.

'And that's all right, Svea,' he said, holding her face in his hands. 'If you're worried about my feelings on the matter, I'm fine with it. *You* are all I need.' He kissed her lightly on the lips and allowed his hands to roam down her back again. He pulled her close. 'Now, where were we...?'

'The thing is,' she said, resting her hands on his chest, pushing him back gently so he fell onto the bed. She unclasped the brooch on the other side of her dress, letting the whole thing drop to her waist, and then she continued to push the garment down to the floor. 'I can't be sure, but I think I may be...'

'With child...' he gasped, taking in her beautiful body, including her rounded stomach. He looked stunned—shocked, even.

'I was worried about telling you, knowing your feelings...'

And then his eyes met hers, and she saw they were glowing with love and admiration. Suddenly his arms wrapped around her stomach, pulling her towards him.

He planted a gentle, chaste kiss on her swollen belly. 'That was then...this is now.'

When he was inside her, he stopped for just a moment, looking down into her eyes. 'Is this a risk?' he asked, concerned. 'To you or the baby?'

'No, thank goodness!' She laughed. 'Because there's no way I could stay away from your touch for so long...'

He grinned as he began to move inside her again, deeply, intimately. 'Thank you for helping me to love myself, Svea. I want you to know that this child will be loved, too—just like you will be—for the rest of our lives.'

'You both smell of the sea,' she said.

'We've been making great big fortresses out of the sand on the beach,' Ash said.

'He's going to be just like his father!' She laughed, thinking of the wonderful settlement Ash had built here in Braewood. 'He's going to create great things. Perhaps you'll do it together.'

Ash grinned. 'I hope so. Ellette is about to take Bearn for his bath. Do you feel like a walk? It's a beautiful evening.'

Svea nodded. 'All right. Just give me a moment to finish.'

The sun was beginning to set in the distant sky, and there was a glorious patchwork of pink and orange clouds floating above them. Svea was surprised when, instead of taking her down their usual favourite path to the beach, where they often enjoyed a moonlit swim together, Ash took her hand and led her through the settlers' farmsteads, past the barns and towards the crop fields.

'Where are we going?'

'I have something for you. Or rather, I have made something for you.'

She looked up at him, a wide, expectant smile on her face. 'What is it?'

'Come this way and I'll show you,' he said, tugging her through a low wall and into a field of...

She gasped.

Stretched out before her was a field full of hundreds and hundreds of beautiful sunflowers, their large, happy-looking faces all turning towards them

'When I came back to Braewood after the battle I came here to think. I came across this ancient tree and I realised why I'd always been drawn to you, and to your patterns,' he said, trailing his fingertips over the swirls on her body that matched those in the canopy above them. 'I realised that from the moment I first saw you on the battlefield we were connected somehow. That you were my home.'

And as Ash made love to her under the canopy of the tree, taking her to new realms of pleasure, sowing a new seed inside her, she knew there would be many more generations of their family to come. A mixture of Saxon and Dane.

In many, many years from now, in the distant future, Svea and Ash would no longer be here, but she hoped that they would have left a legacy. This tree with all its roots and memories…Svea's chronicles for people to read and decipher…a family. But mostly she knew that theirs would be a great legacy of love.

* * * * *

If you enjoyed this story, be sure to read the other book in the Rise of the Ivarssons miniseries

The Viking's Stolen Princess

And look out for more great books from Sarah Rodi, coming soon!